The Arranger

Amish Country Brides

~

Jennifer Spredemann

Get a FREE Amish story as my thank you gift
when you sign up for my newsletter here:
www.jenniferspredemann.com

OTHER

Learning to Love – Saul's Story (Sequel to
Chloe's Revelation)
Her Amish Identity
An Unexpected Christmas Gift

COMING 2023 (Lord Willing)

A Widower's Amish Courtship
A Christmas Amish Courtship
Special 10 Year Anniversary Edition of
Amish by Accident
The Crimson Dress (previously published under a
pen name)
The Wanderer (Amish Country Brides)

BOOKS by J.E.B. SPREDEMANN
AMISH GIRLS SERIES

Joanna's Struggle
Danika's Journey
Chloe's Revelation
Susanna's Surprise
Annie's Decision
Abigail's Triumph
Brooke's Quest
Leah's Legacy
A Christmas of Mercy – Amish Girls Holiday

Unofficial Glossary
of Pennsylvania Dutch Words

Ach – Oh

Ach du liebe – Expression similar to "Oh, my goodness!" or "Oh, dear!"

Bann – Shunning/excommunication

Boppli/Bopplin – Baby/Babies

Bruder/Brieder – Brother/Brothers

Daed/Dat – Dad

Denki – Thanks

Der Herr – The Lord

Der Welt – The world

Dietsch – Pennsylvania German

Dochder(n) – Daughter(s)

Dumm – Dumb

Dummkopp – Dummy

Englischer – A non-Amish person

Ferhoodled – Crazy, scatterbrained, mind is elsewhere

Fraa – Wife/Missus

G'may – Members of an Amish fellowship

Gott – God

Gross sohn – Grandson

Gut – Good

Haus – House

Herr – Mister/Lord

Hochmut – Proud

Jah – Yes

Kapp – Amish head covering for women

Kinner – Children

Kumm – Come

Lieb – Love

Maed/Maedel – Girls/Girl

Mamm – Mom

Nee – No

Ordnung – Rules followed by the Amish church (varies according to district)

Schatzi – Sweetheart

Schweschder(n) – Sister(s)

Sohn – Son

The familye way – Pregnant

Vatter – Father

Verboten – Forbidden

Wunderbaar – Wonderful

Author's Note

The Amish/Mennonite people and their communities differ one from another. There are, in fact, no two Amish communities exactly alike. It is this premise on which this book is written. I have taken cautious steps to assure the authenticity of Amish practices and customs. Old Order Amish and New Order Amish may be portrayed in this work of fiction and may differ from some communities. Although the book may be set in a certain locality, the practices featured in the book may not necessarily reflect that particular district's beliefs or culture. This book is purely fictional and built around a fictional community, even though you may see similarities to real-life people, practices, and occurrences.

We, as *Englischers*, can learn a lot from the Plain People and their simple way of life. Their hard work, close-knit family life, and concern for others are to be applauded. As the Lord wills, may this special culture continue to be respected and remain so for many centuries to come, and may the light of God's salvation reach their hearts.

PROLOGUE

*L*ucy Bontrager was hiding a secret.

If *Dat*, aka Bishop Jerry Bontrager to the rest of *g'may*, ever got wind of her activities this summer, he'd probably ground her for life. Seriously.

But Lucy couldn't help spending time with handsome Trey Montgomery. From the moment they'd first spoken in the dollar store, she knew she was in trouble.

She wasn't even sure what it was about him. *Jah*, he was funny—or silly was more like it. But she'd been flattered to catch the attention of a *gut*-looking *Englisch bu. Nee, Englisch* man. She'd known he was *verboten*, but that hadn't stopped her from agreeing to meet him at the coffee shop in town a few days after they'd met. Nor had it prevented her from joining him for lunch and ice cream. Or stealing away with him at his house and riding in his car.

It had been a bad idea from the start, but she couldn't seem to help herself.

Dat wouldn't be happy one bit. Especially if he knew Trey was a soldier.

Ach, what had she gotten herself into?

~

Trey coaxed Lucy onto his lap, pressing his lips to the side of her head. "I'm going to miss you when I'm gone, you know."

"Gone?" She pulled back, her eyes searching his. "What do you mean? Where are you going?"

He stroked her hair, something he'd complimented her on many times. He loved it when she removed her *kapp* and allowed her hair to fall free. He loved running his fingers through it. *She* loved when he ran his fingers through it. "I told you, remember? I'm in the military, babe. I have to take my tour of duty."

"I don't know what that means."

"I have to go wherever they send me. It's not called *the service* for nothing. I'm serving my country, *our* country." He'd tried to explain this to her before, but it always seemed to go over her head. To her thinking, serving had an entirely different meaning.

She recognized the familiar pride in his voice when he talked about being a soldier. He'd once told her he couldn't help being proud, and that not all pride was a bad thing.

It had been strange hearing a different point of view other than the one she'd grown up learning. Did the Bible ever talk about pride being a *gut* thing? *Nee.* She didn't think so.

It was what made the devil fall, *ain't not*? Trey had laughed when she'd told him that, so she wouldn't mention it again. She hadn't thought it was funny in the least.

"*Fools make a mock at sin.*" She could hear *Dat's* voice quoting the Scripture verse now. He'd mentioned it many a time when one of her *brieder* would speak nonchalantly about the shenanigans some of the *youngie* indulged in.

Lucy frowned. "Where are they sending you?"

He shrugged. "That's the thing. I don't know. But I doubt it'll be much worse than bootcamp. Most likely it'll be a foreign country, helping keep the peace."

She didn't like when Trey spoke of things she knew little about. It was almost like he spoke a different language.

He rubbed her back and began lightly massaging her shoulders. She'd miss his capable hands, for sure. Trey's touch was something she didn't think she'd ever tire of. "Don't you worry, beautiful. I'd be happy to give my life for this country."

She gasped. "Give your life?"

"There's no guarantee I'll return. Some of these missions are dangerous. It's the risk I took when I signed up, Luce." She'd always liked his nickname for her.

She leaned back and stared into the eyes that always made her forget all her worries and remember why she'd fallen for him in the first place. She loved the way his skin crinkled at the corners when he smiled. She adored the faint freckles against his tanned skin. Trey was hard to resist. "When will you return from this tour?"

"It'll actually be more like a mission."

He kept saying *mission*. Isn't that what *Englisch* churches did? She doubted Trey meant the same thing. From what she knew, the churches went in to do good things. They didn't drive tanks and tote guns.

"I'm not sure how long I'll be gone. It'll probably be at least a year or more, I'm thinking. Unless something happens to me. I'm not really worried about that, though. Whatever happens will happen. I can't control my destiny."

"But they didn't force you to become a soldier, did they?

"No. I volunteered of my own free will. You know that I'm proud of what I do. I just wish *you* were too. Someone has to defend our country."

She had so many questions. Was the country in danger of being attacked? She hadn't seen or heard anything from any of the newspapers *Dat* read. Surely, he would have mentioned something if they were in danger. And if they weren't, why did the country need defending?

Wouldn't *Der Herr* protect them? And if not, His will would be done. If anything happened, bad or *gut*, it was because *Gott* allowed it. Otherwise, He would have prevented it. That's what she'd always believed and had been taught.

But she wouldn't ask Trey those kinds of questions. It was difficult being in a relationship with someone you didn't see eye to eye with. Perhaps it had been a mistake getting involved with Trey.

She cast the thought aside. She didn't want to think those thoughts right now. Not while she was being held in Trey's strong arms. Not when his warm lips caressed hers. Not when she was too distracted to think about anything but the handsome *Englisch* man in front of her.

ONE

*L*ucy's fingers trembled as she held the plastic device in her hands. She stared down at it in disbelief. Two blue lines. *Ach*, this could not be. It couldn't. She was the bishop's *dochder*. She couldn't be in the *familye* way. Especially not with an *Englischer's boppli*.

Nee. Tears rushed to the surface, threatening to spill over her lashes and onto her cheeks. *Take a deep breath*, she told herself. *It's going to be okay. It'll work out*. Somehow.

But would it, really?

Her father had been watching her again this morning as she'd completed her chores. He had to know something was up when she'd retched after entering the barn two mornings in a row. Her stomach couldn't handle the offensive odors that accompanied farm life, even though she been around them her entire eighteen-year existence.

Dat had asked her what was wrong, but she couldn't bear to tell him what she'd suspected. Now, the truth had been confirmed. Now, she would *have* to tell *Dat*. Now, her life would be changed. Forever.

For sure and certain, she'd need to get a message to Trey. Somehow. How would he react? Would he offer to marry her? Would he become Amish? *Nee*, she didn't think so. He still had three more years of service to the military, which was something he couldn't get out of if he wanted to. At least, that was what he'd told her before he'd been deployed overseas two weeks ago.

Ach, she should have never given in to his pleas. He'd wanted to be sure she was his girl, he'd said. He'd wanted to have something to remember her by when he was away, he'd said. He'd wanted her to commit to him with her whole heart, he'd said.

And she had. She'd given him everything. But now that she had time to think, *he* hadn't given *her* everything. *Jah*, he'd promised his love. *Jah*, he'd promised he'd think of her every day while he was gone. *Jah*, he'd promised to remain faithful. But he hadn't promised that she wouldn't end up carrying his *boppli* while he was thousands of miles away. He hadn't promised to marry her. He hadn't promised her a happily-ever-after. *Nee*, this was anything but.

This was terrifying.

Dat hadn't even known she'd been dating an *Englischer*. As far as her father knew, she'd been faithfully attending the Amish youth gatherings on the weekends. She'd simply been going to the store to get groceries and what not.

Not meeting in secret with her *Englisch* beau.

Ach, what had she done?

A knock on the bathroom door startled her.

"Lucy, are you okay in there?" *Mamm* asked.

Nee. No, she was not okay. Not in the least.

"*Jah*." She lied. "I'll be out in a minute."

She hurried but fumbled with the pregnancy test. What should she do with it and the box it had come in? She rifled through the bathroom cabinet and found an empty plastic grocery bag, then she wasted several squares of toilet paper to wrap around the test and hide any evidence. She would close the plastic bag tightly, then chuck it into the trash can.

The evidence was now gone, but her predicament remained the same. She, the bishop's daughter, had become pregnant out-of-wedlock with an *Englischer's* baby.

What on earth was she going to do?

~

The last thing Lucy expected as she entered the barn was to find her father standing between the stalls, his arms crossed over his chest, his lips turned downward, and holding her positive pregnancy test in his hand.

His steely gaze fixed on hers. "I think we need to talk."

Ach, her chest was going to cave in on her. She couldn't breathe. She couldn't move. Without permission, tears and a sob escaped her, and she hung her head in shame. "I'm sorry, *Dat*!"

In a split second, her father's arms were around her. In all her life, she couldn't remember her father ever pulling her into an embrace. "We will take care of this, *dochder*. We will find a solution."

After the trembling subsided and her tears had dried, her father released her.

"I don't know what to do, *Dat*." She brushed away a stray tear.

"I know you are scared right now, but you are not the first to be in this predicament."

She was pretty sure she was the only Amish girl in *this* district to be in *this* predicament. *Dat* had no idea. And she wasn't looking forward to sharing the whole truth with him or anyone else. What kind of a girl would they think she was?

"You must marry the *bu*. Who is it? One of the Stoltzfus boys?"

"*Nee.*"

Dat paced back and forth, then scratched his head and frowned. "Not Silas Miller's *bu.*"

"*Nee. Dat*, you don't know him."

He stopped pacing and stared at her. Lucy thought he might be looking straight into her soul. She saw even more disappointment etched in his features. "You've been seeing someone from *Detweiler's, ain't not?*"

Dat thought he understood, but he hadn't a clue about the mess she'd managed to make. He was pretty good at guessing and she'd understand his concerns about being in the *familye* way with someone from Detweiler's district, since the two districts weren't permitted to mix. *Dat* had never had a problem with their *g'may* intermarrying with Detweiler's, but since their neighboring district's leaders had decided against it, then *Dat* as bishop, would respect their wishes. And if his *dochder were* in this situation, it would present some challenges and cause even more friction between the two Plain communities.

But that, of course, was *not* the case.

"*Nee, Dat..*" *Ach*, it pained her to even utter the words. Because her situation was *much much* worse than her father had imagined. She took a deep breath, knowing her next words would not go over well.

"It was an *Englischer*." Her voice was nearly a whisper.

At the admission, her father stumbled back, eventually falling onto a bale of hay.

Oh, goodness.

"*Dat*! Are you all right?" If she'd caused her father to have a heart attack, she'd never forgive herself.

"What have you done, *dochder*? When...? How...? An *Englischer*, Lucinda?" *Ach*, she hated when *Dat* or *Mamm* referred to her by her full name.

"I'm sorry, *Dat*. I never thought...but we..." There was really nothing she could say to rectify this situation.

Dat shook his head and swatted the air. "*Ach*, I guess it doesn't matter now. What's done is done." He rubbed his forehead and sighed heavily. "Is there *any* chance he would become Amish?"

She wasn't sure why he'd even asked, since their district didn't readily accept *Englischers* into their fold. But perhaps they'd make an exception since she was the bishop's *dochder*. Or maybe for her situation? "He isn't even in the country. He's a soldier, *Dat*. I have no idea when he will return from wherever they sent him."

"A *soldier*?" *Dat* covered his eyes. "Did you set out to defy *every* rule our community has put forth? Everything our people have stood for for centuries?

Lucy, I am the bishop! Do you have *any* idea how this will look to our people? Why didn't you think first?"

Ach, she hated hearing her father's reprimand, but he was one hundred percent right. She had not been thinking about the consequences her choices would bring. She hadn't thought of any of it. All she'd thought about was loving Trey and making him happy and how *gut* it felt to be in his arms. She'd never imagined she would end up alone and in the *familye* way.

She lifted her head hoping *Dat* would read her sincerest apology in her eyes. There was really nothing she could say to make this better.

"Well, what are you planning to do now?" He demanded.

"I don't know. I haven't had time to think about it yet." She hadn't even seen her best friend Shiloh since she'd discovered the news. But even if she had, she didn't know if she'd tell Shiloh or not. Although, at this point, it might be nice to have a sympathetic ear and someone to ask advice from.

"I will contact your *Onkel*, then. We will send you to my *Englisch* brother's to—"

"*Nee, Dat*! Please. Don't send me away." Her entire body shook now. She couldn't bear enduring an entire pregnancy alone. And among *Englisch* strangers? The thought was terrifying. "I don't want to go away."

"It is better if you give this child up and move on with your life. No one needs to know about this."

"*Nee*. I could never." She adamantly shook her head and the tears tumbled down her apron. "Please, *Dat*. Let me keep the *boppli*."

Grief marred *Dat's* face. Lucy hated what this was doing to him. She was certain the stress must be decreasing his lifespan. As though his position as bishop weren't challenging enough.

"I...I need to pray. I must seek *Der Herr's* will in this." He ambled to the tack room, then turned before shutting himself inside. "You will mention this to *no* one. Do you hear me? No one."

She nodded. "Okay."

"You must pray too."

Ach, she was too ashamed to go before *Der Herr* now, but she nodded, nonetheless.

At that, her father closed the door. Chances were, he'd lock himself inside until *Der Herr* provided an answer. She only hoped it would come soon.

TWO

When Justin Beachy heard footsteps approaching his shop, he turned his head toward the entry door. He slid out from under the buggy he'd been working on, then wiped his hands on a shop towel. His grin widened and he stretched out his hand as his friendly bishop approached. "Hello, Jerry. What brings you by today? Need a new buggy?"

A frown carved lines into the bishop's face. "If only it was as simple as that." He glanced around the quiet shop. "Do you have a few minutes?"

"*Jah*, sure." He sensed unease in the bishop's demeanor.

"Could we go somewhere more private?" Jerry asked.

Justin gestured behind them. "Is my office okay?"

"*Jah*, that should do."

Justin led the way and motioned to the chairs

across from his desk. "You may have a seat, if you'd like."

Jerry nodded. "*Denki.*"

Justin sat in his leather office chair, as unease crawled through his veins. What on earth could the bishop have to discuss that required privacy?

The bishop's hands clenched and unclenched, and he blew out a breath. "I'm sure you're wondering what has me all worked up."

"Have I done something wrong?" Usually, it would be the deacon that confronted such matters. For the life of him, though, he couldn't come up with any rules he may have broken.

"*Nee.* At least nothing I'm aware of." Jerry drew in another long breath, then expelled it. "Before we begin this conversation, I need to know that I can trust you. Nothing that we say can pass these four walls."

"You have me worried, Jerry." He thought about cracking a joke about hoping the bishop didn't want him to help bury a body to cut the tension in the room, but he sensed this wasn't the time.

"It is a very personal matter that I have been praying about. Every time I do, *Der Herr* brings you to mind, so I'm thinking you're the one."

"I'm the...?" Justin shook his head. "You're being quite vague."

"This is very important to me. Until I have assurance you will not utter this to anyone—"

"You have my promise."

"You're sure?"

"If it's that important to you, then yes, I will keep it to myself. I'm just wondering, why you've come to me." The bishop had never confided in him before.

"And that is the matter I am getting to." The bishop wiped his hands on his pantlegs.

Ach, Justin had never seen their district leader so vulnerable.

"You see, my *dochder*...she..." Jerry's words came out as a sob.

"What is wrong with her? Which *dochder*?" Not that he even knew Jerry's daughters by name. He hadn't been in this district all that long, although, he'd tried to remember who was who.

The bishop wiped away his tears. "The youngest. Lucy, she's...*ach*, I can hardly even say the words. She's...in a situation."

Justin's brow furrowed. What on earth was the bishop trying to communicate? "A situation?"

"A predicament, actually. She just found out that she is expecting a *boppli*. With an *Englischer*." Jerry hung his head at the words.

Justin understood good and well what it meant

17

when someone left the Amish church and became *Englisch*. In the Amish community where he'd grown up in Pennsylvania, they'd believed that leaving the Amish doomed one to certain hell.

"*Ach*." What was he supposed to say to that? He had no idea. "I'm sorry."

"*Jah*, me too."

He still had no clue why the bishop was sharing his woes with him. "What...I mean, why are you sharing this with me? I'm confused." Because if he was hoping to keep it a secret...none of this was adding up

Jerry raised his eyes to meet Justin's. "This *Englischer* is not around, but even if he was..." Jerry shook his head. "What I'm trying to say is I was hoping you would briefly court and marry my *dochder*. Soon."

A punch in the gut would have been more expected—and welcomed—than the words the bishop had just spoken. "Wait. You..." He scratched his chin, attempting to wrap his mind around the bishop's ludicrous proposal. He couldn't be serious, could he? Was he stuck in dream, or nightmare? He wasn't sure which one? He shook his head. "Listen, Jerry I—"

"I'm *begging* you, Justin." His teary eyes evidenced his words.

"You're serious." All of a sudden, his throat felt dry. "Why *me*?"

"You're a *gut* Amish man. I've watched you. I trust you. You are older. You are already established with a place of your own. And I know you would treat the *boppli* as your own and you'd treat my *dochder* well."

It was true. He was all those things, but... "I'm honored that you have that much faith in me. Truly." He squeezed his eyes shut. "May I have some time to process this? To think? And pray?"

"Of course." The bishop seemed visibly relieved. Was it because he hadn't outright rejected the crazy notion? He'd certainly wanted to.

This was a lot to process.

"Okay, let me think for a minute here." Justin rubbed his forehead. "Your *dochder* Lucy is in the *familye* way. With an *Englischer's boppli*." He stood up and paced behind his desk. "What about the *Englischer*?"

"He doesn't know about the *boppli*. No one does. Right now, it's me, you, and Lucy."

"Her *mamm* doesn't even know?" He felt like his eyes might jump out of their sockets.

"I thought that if the two of you courted...and then she was in the *familye* way..." Jerry shrugged.

"So, you'd want me to pretend the *boppli* is mine." He said flatly. "Do you know how much I've wanted to redeem my family's name after my *brieder*...? *Ach*,

Jerry. I don't know if I can do this. Maybe if I wasn't a Beachy, but—"

"Don't you see? That's what makes you the perfect candidate. No one would think twice about a *boppli* if a Beachy is involved." He was right, of course.

Justin palmed his forehead. *Candidate?* It made him feel like he was running for public office. "How old is your *dochder*?"

"She just turned eighteen."

"Eighteen!" He hadn't meant to shout the word, but for goodness' sake. *Eighteen?* "No way."

"I know you have to be about—"

"Past thirty. Can you imagine how people would talk? I'd be labeled the worst Beachy yet. A cradle robber. And of the bishop's *dochder*, no less." His heart clenched.

"I hadn't considered that, really." Jerry sighed heavily. "All I know is that when I prayed for a solution, *Der Herr* brought you to mind. More than once."

"You think this is something *Gott* wants me to do?" He hadn't considered *Der Herr* asking him to sacrifice his reputation. Was he being too prideful? He didn't think so. Wasn't a *gut* name rather to be chosen than great riches? "But pretending the *boppli* is mine would be dishonest."

"I would never ask you to lie. And I'm pretty certain most people aren't going to ask."

"And if they do?" Because *he* was pretty sure his family would have something to say about it. To go from bachelor to marrying the bishop's pregnant *dochder* was going to raise some brows. He wasn't sure his family would buy it. Especially Joshua. But he and Josh hadn't been as close as they once were.

"Like I said, how you respond will be on you. Just, if you *do* happen to tell someone, ask them to keep it a secret."

"What does your *dochder* think of all this?"

"Lucy has no idea I'm talking to you. But I told her I would help her find a solution."

Ach du liebe. "Well, that's great. She'll probably take one look at me and flee for the hills."

"Nonsense. She will do as I advise her. She really is a *gut* girl. She just doesn't always make the best decisions." Jerry grimaced.

You think? Thank *Gott* he'd had enough sense to keep that comment to himself. *Barely eighteen?* That meant she had two years of being a teenager yet. *Ach.*

"I know that I promised you I wouldn't tell anyone, but—" He left off talking at the bishop's frown. "It's just that I *really* need to talk to Sammy. I tell him everything and he advises me. He's not even in this district and I know he wouldn't tell a soul if I asked him not to."

The bishop seemed to be contemplating his words. "I know Sammy Eicher. He will offer sound, Godly advice. You may share it with him *only*."

Just hearing those words lifted about ten pounds off his shoulders.

The bishop tapped the desk. "When do you think you can have an answer for me?"

"I'm not sure. But I would want to speak with your *dochder* as well. I don't know her at all. Honestly, I'm not even sure which *maedel* she is."

He realized how bad his admission probably sounded to the bishop, but he tried not to make a habit of staring at young women. He believed that *Der Herr* would bring him a *fraa* when the time was right. *Gott, is this Your time?*

Jerry nodded. "I can bring her by tomorrow, if that suits you."

"Tomorrow." He blew out a long breath. He might be meeting his *fraa* tomorrow. Had the temperature risen a notch? Because he suddenly felt warm all over.

"If time wasn't of the essence, I wouldn't be rushing this. Or encouraging it."

"I'll speak with Sammy tonight, then." He moved around his desk to walk the bishop out.

"I appreciate it." Jerry clasped Justin's shoulder. "I

realize this is a great sacrifice for you. Do not think *Der Herr* will not reward you for it, *sohn*."

Sohn. Ach, the word made him think of his folks. Just the thought of his parents discovering that the *maedel*—the very young *maedel* and the bishop's *dochder*—he would be courting was in the *familye* way, and them believing it was his *boppli*, sent him reeling. The thought of their disappointment was a heavy burden he didn't even want to think of bearing.

Why me, Gott? *What have I done to deserve this?*

Ach, he should be ashamed of his thoughts. Who was *he* to question *Der Herr's* will? If it were someone other than the bishop who'd approached him, he would have outright refused. But the fact that Jerry had spent time in prayer and *Gott* put *him* on the bishop's heart...who was *he* to say no? How *could* he say no?

Whatever he decided to do, he knew he needed to talk to Sammy. Perhaps Sammy would help him see another side. Another solution. Talk him out of it?

One could only hope.

THREE

"Well, it's an interesting situation for sure." Sammy Eicher, Justin's wise elderly friend, rubbed his wiry beard. "Can't say I've ever encountered anything like this before."

"Sammy, I honestly don't know what to do about this." Justin's hand slid through his hair. "I mean, I do feel bad for the girl."

"Have you taken any time to get to know her?"

"No, I can't even...this really isn't what I planned for my future. It's not how I thought my life would go."

"Maybe God has different thoughts than you do." Sammy's eyebrow arched as he sipped his lemonade. "Why don't you allow GOD to write your life story? He's a better writer than you are. Have you ever considered His hand might be in this?"

"I did, but...How can that be?"

"You know, this might sound funny, but your situation kind of reminds me of another one I've read about." Sammy's head bobbed.

"Okay." He wondered where his friend was going with this. "The thing is, I hate to drag the Beachy name through the mud. Again."

"I see. Well, this other situation that I was thinking about, it was similar to yours in a way."

"Do I know these people?"

"Personally? *Nee*. Not yet, anyhow."

"Are you planning to introduce me to them? Because I don't really have a lot of time. The bishop was hoping for my answer tomorrow. He was going to bring his *dochder* by."

"I cannot introduce you because I have not met him either. But I do know his Son." Sammy's eyes met his. "I believe you do too."

Justin wrinkled his brow. "Who is it?"

"Jesus."

"Jesus?"

"*Jah.* Just think about the circumstance of His birth. Joseph found out that Mary was pregnant with a *boppli* that wasn't his."

"But he was going to divorce her, right?"

"It would have been similar to a divorce. In that day, to break up after you were betrothed was a pretty scandalous thing." Sammy lifted a finger. "But Joseph didn't 'put her away' as the Bible says."

"*Nee*, but an angel spoke to him and told him it was okay to marry her. Her child was conceived by the Holy Ghost. *This* is hardly the same thing." He didn't want to sound judgmental toward Lucy, but the facts were the facts.

"That is true. But have you thought of Joseph's reputation? His intended being with child, although they were not married yet? I assure you, it was a bigger deal back then and in that culture than it is today. If Joseph were to have abandoned her and claimed she was expecting another man's child, there was a *gut* chance she could have been put to death."

"So, do you think people believed Jesus was Joseph's biological son?"

Sammy chuckled. "I reckon that would have been easier for them to believe than a virgin birth. Remember when Jesus spoke and those around Him were amazed at His wisdom? They mentioned Him being the carpenter's son. So, *jah*, I think there's a *gut* chance they thought Joseph to be His father."

Justin contemplated Sammy's words. If what he said was true, then just like Justin, Joseph might have pretended the child was his own. And just like Justin, Joseph would have sacrificed his reputation—not only for the *gut* of Mary and her *boppli*, but for good of the entire human race. "My sacrifice wouldn't be as noble."

"Maybe not, but it is admirable that you're considering it."

"What would *you* do, Sammy?"

"Well, first I'd pray and seek *Der Herr's* will in the matter."

"I don't think I've stopped praying since the bishop left. That's why I'm here."

"Other than your reputation, is there a reason why you wouldn't agree to it?"

"I feel like there are a hundred reasons. It's not my *boppli*. What about the other guy?"

"You said he doesn't know, right?"

"Correct. But is it right on her part not to tell him? If I had a child, I'd want to know."

"But you said he's far away."

"Jerry said he's in another country and she has no idea when or if he'll return."

"It's a predicament indeed." Sammy played with the condensation on his lemonade glass.

"Another thing. She's only eighteen. Practically a *boppli* herself. Wouldn't it just be wrong?"

"If she is in the *familye* way, I assure you she is not a *boppli*. Eighteen is considered an adult in the

Englisch world. She may just be more experienced in some things than you are." Sammy's brow arched.

Heat enveloped Justin and trickled down to his toes. "*Ach, jah,* you're right. I haven't...I mean, I've never..." *Jah,* he'd just leave off talking right there.

"Have you thought about what you have to offer the *maedel* and the *boppli*? Perhaps you can be a blessing to them. And what about you? Have you never considered having a family of your own?"

"*Jah.* I just thought it would look...*different.* More normal, I guess."

"Love seldom looks the way we imagine."

Love? He hadn't really thought about *loving* them, just meeting their needs.

Sammy continued, "It might be awkward at first, but before you know it, life together will become as ordinary as waking up to sunshine. And then when the two of you have *bopplin* that you've created, you'll wonder why you stayed single for so long." Sammy grinned.

Ach, he hadn't thought about the future. He could only think of the here and now. But Sammy was right. This part of his life might be difficult, but it wouldn't last forever.

"Sammy?" Justin took a deep breath. "Would you pray for me? For us?"

"I will."

"I've never been a husband or father before. I feel inadequate. I'm just so scared that I'm going to mess things up."

"And how would you go about doing that?"

"I don't know." He shrugged. "But the fear is there just the same."

"Remember, it is not *Gott* who gives the spirit of fear. That comes from the evil one."

"I'm just wondering, why me?" He lifted his palms.

"Why *not* you?"

Justin rubbed his forehead. "I don't know. I just know everyone's going to flip when they hear the news. My *brieder* will give me a hard time for sure and certain."

"They have no stones to throw."

"Right." He sucked in a calming breath. "What do *you* think I should do?"

Sammy raised his hands. "I will not tell you how to decide. That has to come from *Der Herr*. But know that whatever you decide, I will support you."

"*Denki.* I really appreciate your friendship." With Sammy's support and the bishop's, would the situation really be that bad?

All he could think of was to pray that it wouldn't.

FOUR

*L*ucy startled when she turned to go downstairs. "*Dat*. I didn't see you there." Her hand flew to her heart.

"I wanted to catch you while your *mamm* was out with the laundry." Had she ever seen *Dat's* demeanor so serious?

"*Jah*, I was going to help her." She finished tying on her apron.

"*Nee*. Not right now, *dochder*." His hand settled on her shoulder and his stare bore into her as he whispered, "I've found a solution for your situation."

Lucy swallowed hard as dread filled her. Who knew what "solution" *Dat* may have found? All she knew was that she didn't want to have to go away by herself. She didn't want to live with *Englisch* strangers she'd never met, even if they were kin. *Anything* would be better than that, wouldn't it? "Wha...What is it?" Her hands trembled.

"I found a *gut* Amish man who I think will take you as his *fraa*." *Dat* nodded in satisfaction.

Oh no. She raked her mind searching for who *Dat* might have possibly found. What kind of man would agree to marry her on such short notice? "Who?"

"Justin Beachy."

Lucy couldn't help her sharp intake of breath. *Justin Beachy?* Oh my. She needed a fan. Or one of those fainting couches she'd once read about in an old book. How on earth had *Dat* managed to rope their community's most eligible—and handsome—bachelor into marrying *her*?

"I realize he is quite a bit older than you, but he will make a *gut* husband. You'll see." He patted her hand.

"He agreed?" She squeaked out the words. Just the thought of being married to Justin Beechy made her weak in the knees. She should probably sit down a spell.

"He said he would pray about it. I'm certain he will agree." His eyes searched hers. "We will go see him later today. He is expecting us."

~

Lucy had been lost in thought since she and *Dat* had begun the journey to Justin Beachy's homestead. She'd tried quelling the butterflies swarming in her belly, to no avail.

If she were honest with herself, she would admit that she was nervous about speaking with Justin Beachy. If she were honest with herself, she would admit that she used to have a secret crush on Justin Beachy. If she were honest with herself, she would admit that the possibility of Justin Beachy courting and marrying her brought a measure of comfort and excitement to her soul.

The thing was, when she'd met Trey, she'd all but forgotten about her fanciful musings of the older handsome bachelor. When Justin first arrived in the community, she and her friends would tease each other, dreaming that he would ask one of them if they'd like a ride home. He never had.

In all fairness, though, he may have considered them too young. She thought she had caught his eye a time or two, but to her disappointment, nothing ever came of it. She hoped the reason wasn't because he didn't find her attractive. Because, if she ended up married to the man, she'd want him to find her irresistible.

Although he'd attended the youth gatherings for a while when he'd been new in the community, he eventually stopped going. That was around the time Lucy had met Trey at one of the local stores. Trey was friendly and charming and quite *gut*-looking, and

Lucy was immediately attracted to his plentiful smiles. No doubt, his *boppli* would be handsome as well. She'd thought she loved him, but somewhere deep inside, she'd known a relationship between them wouldn't work out in the end. Thinking back now on her gut feeling, she wished she wouldn't have given herself away to him. A part of her was saddened that Trey would never know his child. And even though her father insisted on keeping her *boppli* a secret, she felt guilty not entertaining plans to tell Trey about his *boppli* when he returned home from overseas. He had a right to know, didn't he? The *boppli* was his too.

But she knew *Dat*. He was terrified of losing her—or any of his *kinner*—to *der welt*. Like he'd lost his older *bruder*. Once *Onkel* Lawrence had left the community, her father had never seen him again. As a matter of fact, Lucy had never even met her uncle. Which made her wonder about something. Why would *Dat* suggest sending her to his *bruder's* house, if he hadn't heard from him in years? Had he hoped to reconnect? Did *Dat* secretly keep in touch with his fence-jumping *bruder*? Or had *Dat* planned to track his brother down, somehow?

Whatever the case may be, it had sparked Lucy's interest. Maybe she'd do some snooping when she was home alone. *If* she was ever home alone.

"Are you ready to meet your soon-to-be husband?" *Dat* asked.

She stuffed her fingernail between her teeth. "I don't...what if he finds me...lacking?"

"He is a *gut* man. I'm sure you will suit him *chust* fine, *dochder*." He shot her a sideways glance from his perch behind the reins. "I will leave you there for a while so you can get acquainted."

Ach. Alone with Justin Beechy. She didn't think she'd ever said more than two words to him. "What should we talk about?" She twisted her apron.

"Whatever you'd discuss with any beau, I reckon. You likely know nothing about each other, so you will have plenty to talk about."

He was right about that. She just hoped Justin liked her.

~

Justin blew out a breath and paced the shop floor. Again.

He'd attempted to work on his buggy orders today but found himself daydreaming. And when he hadn't been daydreaming, he'd made inexcusable blunders. Like trying to attach the back wheel to the front axle. Or cutting the canvas wrong. *Jah*, that mistake had been costly. He decided he was better off not doing anything at all when his brain was all *ferhoodled*.

Never in his life had he been this nervous about seeing a girl. *Nee*, a woman. Because this wasn't just any woman. This woman was to be his *fraa*. Soon.

That meant they'd be living together. Working together. Eating together. Sleeping together. He'd never allowed himself to fantasize about having a *fraa*. But now that the scenario would very likely become a reality, he couldn't help but dwell on the thought. Truth be told, he was crazy with anticipation. But what he *wasn't* anticipating was all the rumors that were sure to soon be flying around the community, nor the disapproving looks aimed at the "Beachy bachelor who took advantage of the bishop's teen *dochder*".

What was, in reality, an act of sacrifice and heroism, would be perceived as an act of selfishness and gratification. He was willing to put himself on the line for the bishop and his *dochder*, though. *Der Herr* knew the truth, and that was what mattered. He just needed to keep reminding himself of that fact so he didn't get cold feet and back out. The bishop was counting on him.

A rattling sound commanded his rapt attention, and his head snapped to the buggy pulling into his driveway. *Ach*, she was here. He briefly closed his eyes. Gott, *please help me.* The short prayer was all he could manage.

He swiped his sweaty palms down the pantlegs of his broadfall trousers, and then realized his *mamm* would soon be relieved of her pant-making duties. *Jah*, having a *fraa* would be a blessing.

He sucked in another calming breath, then stepped outside to greet his guests. The moment the buggy came to a stop at the hitching post, the *maedel* looked his way. *Ach*, she looked familiar. While he didn't think he'd ever spoken to her, he remembered their eyes connecting on occasion. He'd thought her pretty from the moment he saw her, but never considered pursuing a relationship with her because he figured she would think he was too old. But if he had the bishop's full support and his *dochder* agreed, could they make a relationship work between them?

He attempted what he hoped was a smile. His pounding heart had him all *ferhoodled*. His attention never strayed as she exited the buggy and exchanged words with her father. Then the two met him halfway between the hitching post and his shop.

"Justin Beachy, this is my youngest *dochder*, Lucy."

Ach, what should he do? Hug her? Place a holy kiss on her cheek? Offer a handshake? *Nee*, he wasn't thinking straight at all. Instead, he simply nodded. "*Gut* to meet you."

She dipped her head. He hoped she wasn't afraid of him. Or was she just nervous like him?

The bishop looked back and forth between the two of them. "Well, I'll leave you two to get acquainted." He turned to Justin. "I trust you'll bring her home later."

"*Jah*." Justin nodded.

"Very well." The bishop made eye contact with his daughter, then returned to his buggy.

They both watched in awkward silence as Jerry drove out of Justin's driveway.

FIVE

Seconds ticked by in silence... Well, this was awkward.

Justin finally cleared his throat. "Would you like to see my place?" *Soon to be our place.*

"Sure." Lucy's chin trembled. "Um, I...I'm sorry to drag you into my mess." She looked up at him through glassy eyes.

Ach, his heart went out to her. This situation wasn't going to be easy for either of them. "It's all right. I just hope that I can meet your needs. And the *boppli's.*"

Now, a stray tear rolled down her cheek. "You are kind in saying that."

"I mean it." He pivoted and held her gaze. "If your *vatter* prayed and *Der Herr* brought me to his mind, who am I to question *Gott*? It must be His will, ain't so?"

She shrugged. "I suppose."

"I aim to make the best of this situation. I told your *vatter* that I wouldn't outright lie to folks, because I know *Der Herr* would not approve of that. With that being said, I'm okay with people believing this *boppli* is mine. Ours."

Lucy's head lifted and her eyes went wide with astonishment. "You are?"

"*Jah*. And I expect people to judge us. That is just how people are. You can't really blame them. We know the truth and *Der Herr* knows the truth, so that is all that really matters to me. I just want our lives to be pleasing to Him."

"You are a *gut* man, Justin Beachy."

He shook his head once and hard. He didn't want her putting him up on a pedestal. If she'd read his thoughts moments before they'd arrived at his farm, she wouldn't be saying these words. He was a man, after all, and subject to human desires. "I try, but I often fall short."

"Do you truly think *Der Herr* will bless us? After what I've done?"

"That is the beauty of *Der Herr's* grace. It is called amazing grace for a reason. His grace transforms our frailties into our strengths. It turns our failures into our triumphs and our biggest mistakes into our biggest blessings. With Him, I believe we can conquer anything."

She ducked her head. "*Ach*. I am not worthy to be called your *fraa*."

He lifted her chin and stared into her eyes. "Apparently, *Gott* thinks otherwise. And His thoughts are higher than our thoughts. Whatever doubts you have, place them in *Gott's* hands, Lucy. *Kumm*."

When he held out his hand, she placed her delicate fingers into his palm. *Jah*, he was certain *Der Herr* would guide them to the future He had planned.

~

Lucy needed to hug her father. Had he already known how *wunderbaar* Justin Beachy was? As terrible as her situation was, this was probably the best possible outcome.

But she felt horrible that a *gut* honest man like Justin would be bearing the blame for her mistakes. And he certainly would. She could just imagine the gossip now. Especially with their age difference. *Ach*, she really didn't even know how old Justin Beachy was.

"How old are you?" she blurted out, as they meandered toward his house.

He grimaced. "Thirty-three."

"Fifteen years between us then."

"I would have thought your *vatter* would've

chosen someone closer to your own age." He glanced in her direction.

"He trusts you."

"*Jah*. It will cause us much grief, though."

"Like you said, people will talk." She shrugged. "It's really only our business, ain't not? If we don't mind the age difference, they shouldn't either."

His eyes widened. "*You* don't mind?"

She couldn't hide her smile. Who would have thought that tall, strong, gorgeous Justin Beachy would have vulnerabilities? "Did you think I would?"

"*Jah*. Maybe." He shrugged.

"Truth be told, Justin Beachy, I've had a crush on you since the first time I saw you."

His jaw slacked, then he chuckled. "Truly?"

"*Jah*."

Disbelief accompanied his stare. "Why?"

Was he really that clueless? "Have you looked in the mirror? You are every girl's dream."

"I only look in the mirror when I shave." He chuckled. "And I confess that I have no idea what girls' dreams consist of. But I never..." He shook his head. "You're not pulling my leg, are you?"

Lucy laughed. "The Beachy men have a reputation around here."

"*Jah*, I know." He frowned. "It's unfortunate."

"Not that, *bensel*." She bumped his thigh with her hip and laughed. "A reputation for being handsome."

"I hadn't realized. Really?" He grinned.

"*Jah*, really. I think you're pretty hot, Justin Beachy." She winked, knowing her *Englisch* behavior would garner his attention. "But don't let it go to your head."

He chuckled. "Too late. I think my head may have just exploded."

She stopped and stared at him, then reached up and examined his head with her hands. "*Nee*, still there and attractive as ever."

"If you keep talking like that, you are going to have a *hochmut* husband."

"You are the furthest thing from proud that I've seen. And I mean that in a *gut* way."

He held the door open to the house. "This will be your new home soon. I hope you find it tolerable."

Tolerable? She wanted to laugh. "What is wrong with it?"

He shrugged. "It's just that it used to be an *Englisch* home." He pointed across the road. "And don't tell anyone I said this, but the neighbors tend to be a little nosy."

Now she did laugh. "The Millers? Aren't they kin to you?"

"Two of my *brieder* married Miller girls, *jah*."

"But it's only Nathaniel and his *fraa*, Amy, and his folks there now, right?" Her eyes meandered to the property next door, where one of the Miller women worked in the garden. Just as they stepped inside Justin's house, Amy, she guessed, glanced in their direction.

"*Jah*. I'm just worried our relationship won't be believable to them."

"Why wouldn't it be?"

"Because they've never seen me bring a *maedel* home. And trust me, they watch." He glanced through the window.

"Well, then, we're just going to have to make it believable. *Dat* thinks I should come over every day. He suggested you taking me for buggy rides to places other people in the community go. Like Millers' Country Store and Bakery. Make our relationship obvious."

"Your *vatter* said your *mamm* doesn't know?"

"She doesn't. She'll be surprised for sure. *Dat* said I should stay the night here at least once, then have you drop me off in the morning."

His Adam's apple bobbed. "He wants you to...? He said that?"

"He did." She shrugged.

"Well, *that* would certainly make it believable."

"We wouldn't have to do anything. I mean, *Dat* didn't mean for us to."

Pink mottled his neck. "*Ach*, I wouldn't. Not until we're married."

"But we *should* kiss."

His eyes practically jumped out of their sockets. "We should?"

"*Jah*. And let somebody walk in on us."

"I don't—"

"It has to be believable, remember? That will have people talking for certain."

"You're right." He nodded and rubbed the back of his neck, which inadvertently brought her attention to his muscled arm. He cleared his throat. "Should I show you around the place now?"

She smiled at the thought of being the recipient of Justin Beachy's kisses. "Sure."

SIX

Justin watched Lucy as she sat across the porch from him on one of his hickory rockers. From what he had come to know of her so far, he liked her. She definitely had some *Englisch* ways about her. He hadn't expected that from the bishop's *dochder*.

As he'd shown her around the property, she seemed pleased and offered welcome suggestions on how to improve things. He enjoyed hearing a woman's perspective. If she were to become his *fraa*, this would be her place too, and he wanted her to feel at home.

"Will you tell me about the *boppli's* father?" He leaned forward.

She moved the condensation on her tea glass around with her finger and twisted her lips. "What do you want to know about him?"

"How long were you dating? How did you meet?"

"I met him at the dollar store. He put on one of those silly pairs of glasses with the big nose and bushy mustache. He made me laugh." Her smile told him she was probably reliving the moment.

"I see." Justin hoped he'd be able to make her smile that way. He'd always seen himself as the more quiet, serious type. If he was honest with himself, he wasn't sure he'd live up to her expectations. How could he compare to the things she'd likely seen and done in the *Englisch* world?

"We were dating for about six months before he left. Trey's a soldier." She frowned.

"Your father said that he was in another country, but I hadn't realized he was in the military." He leaned forward. "He didn't say when he was supposed to return?"

"*Nee.* I guess he was going on a secret mission. He said he didn't know where he would be, and if he did, he wouldn't be able to tell me anyway. He had no idea how long he'd be gone."

Justin blew out a breath. "So, what happens if he shows up?"

"He won't."

"You sound certain."

"He doesn't know where I live. And if I'm living here with you, he'll have no idea."

"Has he seen you in Amish clothes? Would he be able to recognize you?"

She nodded. "The first time we met, I was wearing Amish clothes. And he saw me a few times after that in my dress and *kapp*."

"Well, I guess there's nothing we can do about that, then. We'll just have to hope he doesn't come looking for you." He met her eyes. "Did you love him? *Do* you love him?"

She twisted her hands in her lap.

"You can be truthful." He encouraged.

"*Jah*, I did. I do. We made a *boppli* together and all." She shrugged then her voice turned somber. "But I don't know how he feels for sure. He said that he loved me, but it could be that he only said it so I would share the marriage bed with him. Or not. I don't know."

"I'm not sure if this is the right thing to do. Us." His finger motioned between the two of them. "Do you?"

She shrugged.

"I feel like I'm moving in on another man's family. If I were in his shoes, and I found out that my beloved married someone else while carrying my *boppli*, I'd be very upset." He shook his head. "*Nee*, I'd be heartbroken."

49

"Trey and I had already talked about the possibility of getting married. And while we both wanted a future together, neither of us were willing to leave our home and culture to be with the other." Her hand moved to her abdomen and a tear slipped down her cheek. "I thought somehow we could make it work, but now I know I was living in a dream world. After he left, I knew there'd be no hope for us. He told me that he'd probably return a different person. War does that to people. I should have never shared the marriage bed with him. I don't know what I was thinking."

"We all do things we aren't proud of."

"*Nee*, not like what I've done." She hung her head.

"No one is perfect." He frowned. "It's just...if he does come back and he wants to continue the relationship..." He sighed.

"Trey and I are over. I can't imagine being apart from my family and friends. I have no desire to become *Englisch*." Her eyes lifted. "If you're worried that I would leave you, you don't need to be. I would never do that."

"I'm not worried about myself. I know *Der Herr* will be with me. I just want *you* to be sure about this. I want you to be happy. Satisfied."

"My biggest fear is being sent away to have this

boppli on my own and having to give it away."

"You will not be sent away. I won't stand for it." He reached over and touched her hand. "You are not alone. I will help you in any way you need me to."

"You will still marry me, then?"

"If you're *sure* that is what *you* want. I don't want you to feel like you're being forced into this. And I don't want you to marry me just because your *vatter* wants it. I want to be sure it is what you want, as well."

She sighed, and he noted the relief in her mien. "It is. *Denki*."

"How long did your *vatter* want you to stay?" He leaned back. "Not that I want you to leave or anything."

"We could go for a drive so people will see us together. We could stop a few places. Timothy and Bailey's greenhouse, Millers' store, Emily's stand."

"*Gut* idea. Do you want to make a list of things? I'm hoping one of these days you might want to make me supper." He winked.

"*Ach*, for sure. Probably many suppers, and other meals too." She nodded. "I like to cook."

"I don't keep much stocked, so we can get whatever you think we'll need."

"If you get me a pen and paper, I can make a list."

"Pen and paper coming up." He shot up from his

chair and snatched their empty glasses in the process. "Would you like a refill?"

She smiled up at him. "Yes, please."

~

Justin Beachy was a dream, Lucy decided. A very lovely dream. Although they would likely be married within the month, she wouldn't allow herself to fantasize about lying in his arms. And he had really nice arms. Among other qualities.

She was looking forward to spending time with this man, who would become her husband. Spending the day with him pleased her in ways she couldn't describe. She desperately hoped he felt the same way about her. Was she just a problem to him, or did he truly enjoy her company? The last thing she wanted was to be an annoyance to him. Of course, he hadn't implied that she might be. But she desired for him to desire her.

"Here you go." Justin stepped outside carrying a glass of tea and a notebook and pen.

"*Denki.*" She took the glass and other things from him.

"*Ach.*" He swept his hair out of his eyes. "It looks like I need to visit *Mamm* soon."

"Because of your hair?" She'd noticed it seemed a little long.

He nodded. "I'm overdue for a haircut, but I've been so busy in the shop lately."

"I could cut it for you." She offered. "We have plenty of time. I've done my *brieder's* hair many times."

"Really? That would be great."

"Do you have a towel and sharp scissors?"

"I do."

"If you fetch them, I can trim your hair before we leave."

"I will. That would be *wunderbaar. Denki.*" His smile stole her breath away. From now on, she determined to bless him any way she could.

~

Justin fumbled around in his kitchen drawer, searching for the sharp scissors he kept handy in the house.

Ach. What had he been thinking?

He hadn't, plain and simple. The more he thought about his future *fraa* trimming his hair, the clammier his hands became. *Mamm* clipping his hair was one thing. But an attractive woman with her gentle hands roaming his face, his neck...her soft fingers feathering through his hair?

He swallowed. *Jah*, this might be a bad idea.

But he couldn't back out now. That would just be

silly. And he didn't want Lucy to believe that he lacked confidence in her abilities.

He headed outside, then realized he'd forgotten the chair and towel. If he was already this *ferhoodled* now, what on earth was he going to be like during the actual hair-cutting session?

When he finally stepped out of the house, his eyes collided with hers. Her bright smile had his heart tripping all over itself. *Ach*, she was a pretty little thing.

He handed over the scissors but couldn't help his trembling fingers.

"*Ach*, are you nervous, Justin?" His name sounded heavenly on her lips.

All coherent words had escaped him, so he nodded.

"It's okay. I won't botch it. I'll do a *gut* job. You'll see." She gestured to the chair. "You may sit."

He admired the confidence in her voice. How could she remain so calm at a time like this?

She opened the towel, draped it over his chest, and brought the corners around to meet at the nape of his neck. Her deft fingers brushed his skin as she tucked the towel under his collar, causing a prickling sensation to shoot through his entire being.

"I should have asked you to get a few more things, it seems." She tapped her lovely pink lips, unwittingly drawing his attention to them. Again.

He stared up at her, mesmerized. Had he ever been this *ferhoodled* in his life?

"I'm going to need a comb and a glass of water," she said.

He began to rise, but her warm hands nudged his shoulders down.

"*Nee*, I can get it. Just tell me where you keep your comb."

His comb. Where did he keep it? His mind drew a blank. *Ach*, he needed to be knocked upside the head with a two-by-four. "The bathroom." He cleared his throat. "In the cabinet."

"I'll be right back. Don't go anywhere." She spun around and hurried into the house. His eyes trailed her until she disappeared out of sight.

He momentarily considered bolting from the chair and locking himself away inside his buggy shop. But then what would he do? He still had to drive her home. He still had to stop by Millers' with her. He still had to pretend like he was madly in love with her.

Pretend?

"All set. You ready now?" Her cheerful voice commanded his attention.

He nodded and allowed her to commence the most frustratingly delicious moments he'd ever had to endure.

SEVEN

As Lucy sat beside Justin in his spring buggy, she couldn't help but notice his warm arm brushing against hers as he guided his driving mare along the road.

His new haircut looked *gut,* despite her getting distracted by his nearness. At one point during his trim, he'd stopped her by catching her hand in his. He hadn't said a word as his thumb had roamed the top of her hand, but his mouth had opened slightly, and his gaze had strayed to her mouth. Had he been thinking about kissing her?

Her heart had hammered in her chest so hard that she was almost certain it could be heard not only by Justin, but by the neighbors across the street too. And maybe Nathaniel Miller *had* heard it. Because when they'd glanced in that direction, he'd been staring at them. She hadn't minded, though. The Millers' seeing them together would aid in their faux courtship.

But Lucy was beginning to realize this courtship might not be fake at all. If she was fortunate enough, perhaps Justin would pleasure her with a kiss at the end of the evening. One could dream.

"What are you thinking about?" His deep voice captured her attention, and drew her back to the present. Had there been a hint of huskiness in it or was that just her imagination?

"I~uh...Nathaniel Miller," she blurted out, flustered. *Jah*, that probably hadn't been the best thing to say. But what was she supposed to say? *I've been daydreaming about you caressing my hand the way you had earlier. Hoping that you might kiss me before the evening is over. Nee*, she couldn't say that aloud.

"If my memory serves me correctly, he's already taken."

Lucy heard the teasing in Justin's tone, but she took the bait anyhow. She feigned offense, then bumped his hip with hers. She wouldn't miss the opportunity to flirt with her future husband. "Not in *that* way, *bensel*. And you should know that *I'm* already taken too." She gave one quick matter-of-fact nod.

A smile danced on his lips. *Ach*, he had a nice smile. And lips. "Is that so?"

"Uh-huh."

"Would I happen to know this lucky fellow?"

"I don't know. Do you?" She arched an eyebrow and boldly set her hand on his pant leg, causing him to flinch and tense under her touch.

"*Ach*!" He quickly removed her hand. "Don't do that." His voice was gruff.

Her cheeks warmed. "I..."

She swallowed hard. Oh, goodness. What had she done? She really needed to get a rein on her *Englisch* habits. Trey had always enjoyed it when she'd made bold moves. "I'm sorry. I didn't mean to upset you."

He turned his head and his wide eyes snapped toward hers. "I didn't say that I didn't *like* it. It's just that..." He gave his head a hard shake. "I don't want to dishonor you, Lucy. And when you do something like that...well, let's just say that it makes me think about and want things I shouldn't. Yet." His gaze slowly swept over her, then he turned his eyes back toward the road and gripped the reins tightly.

Jah, being married to Justin Beachy would be a dream come true, Lucy decided.

~

When Justin walked into Millers' Country Store and Bakery with Lucy at his side, sisters-in-law Kayla and

Jenny Miller were busy behind the counter. The confused looks he and Lucy received when the Miller women looked up almost made him laugh. *Jah*, he guessed seeing the two of them together would spark a bit of controversy. They were an unlikely couple. A Beachy and the bishop's *dochder*.

After greeting the two ladies, he followed behind his future *fraa* as she perused the grocery aisles. Compared to the big-box stores, their offering of consumable items was small, but it was enough to throw together some decent meals. And he didn't know anybody who could stop by the store and not pick up a few delicious treats from the bakery, like Kayla's famous potpie or Jenny's heavenly cinnamon rolls.

He added a few extra items to the basket he carried that hadn't been on the shopping list. Lucy's eyes widened. "You're not going to buy that sugary cereal, are you?"

"Well, I was going to, *jah*." He scratched his cheek then shrugged. "I'm a bachelor."

"Who desperately needs a *fraa*, I see." A shy smile formed on her lips. He loved it when she teased him.

He reached over and twisted her *kapp* tie around one of his fingers then released it, purposely brushing his fingers against her cheek in the process. "I found one." His brow quirked.

Lucy's eyes searched his. "She must be one lucky woman," she whispered.

"*Nee*, I'm the lucky one. But 'blessed' is probably a better word." He lifted his head toward the front of the store, his hand on the small of her back gently encouraging her to walk toward the checkout.

Kayla's gaze bounced back and forth between them. "Did you find everything you need?"

Justin's eyes slid to Lucy. "*Jah*, I did." It appeared that neither Lucy nor Kayla missed the insinuation in his words.

Lucy lightly nudged him with her shoulder. "We wanted something from the bakery too, ain't so?"

"I can get it for you." Jenny Miller offered.

"What do you recommend?" Justin examined the glass bakery cases.

"Today's pretzel day, if you like soft pretzels. Paul loves them." Jenny smiled at the mention of her husband's name.

Justin could only hope that his name would bring a smile to his future *fraa's* lips whenever she spoke it. It had always rubbed him the wrong way when he heard folks talking bad about their spouse. He prayed he would always honor his *fraa*, both in public and in private.

Kayla chuckled beside her. "Paul loves *everything* Jenny makes."

"He likes your potpies, too," Jenny said.

"Everybody likes Kayla's potpies," Lucy remarked. "They are very *gut*."

Kayla bowed her head at the remark. "*Denki*."

Justin eyed Lucy. "Would you like to get one? We could have it for lunch tomorrow."

Lucy nudged him again. Was he giving too much away or was she playing along? "*Jah*, that sounds *gut*."

"Lucy," Kayla said, setting a potpie on the counter. "Shiloh and Sierra are up at the house if you'd like to stop in and say hello."

Lucy looked at Justin, a question in her eyes.

"It's fine with me." He nodded. "Whatever you want to do."

"I'd like to say a quick hello." She looked at Jenny. "Could we get a couple pretzels, please?"

"And a loaf of zucchini bread," Justin added. "I think that'll be it."

Kayla wrung up their groceries and goodies and handed over several bags.

"Would you like some cheese sauce for your pretzels?" Jenny offered.

"None for me, *denki*," Lucy said. "I like them with just salt."

"Me too." Justin winked at Lucy, before the two of them bid their goodbyes.

EIGHT

"*Ach*, I can't believe your boldness!" Lucy said, the moment they stepped out of the store. The windchimes' songs caught her attention as a gentle breeze wafted through them along with the hanging flower baskets that carried the sweet scent of spring.

"We want to be believable, ain't not?" His eyebrow arched. "Besides, I have the Beachy reputation to uphold." He chuckled and shook his head. "I can't believe I just said that."

Lucy giggled. "Well, you're certainly doing a *gut* job. Just wait until Shiloh and Sierra see us together. They're going to flip."

"Did you go to school with them?"

She smiled, thinking of their school days. "*Jah*, they're both *gut* friends."

"Should we put this in the buggy and walk up to

the house, or would you rather drive?"

"I'm a little tired, actually."

His brow creased and concern blanketed his features. "Tired?"

"It's common when you're in the *familye* way. Nothing to worry about." She squeezed his hand.

Justin set the groceries in the back of the buggy, then offered her a hand into the carriage. "How do you know that? Have you already seen the midwife?"

"*Nee*, I was looking through one of *Mamm's* books. I smuggled it up to my room. It's under my mattress." She admitted.

"I see. Maybe I should read this book too."

Lucy nibbled her fingernail. "*Ach*, I don't think so."

"Why not?"

"There are pictures in it." Her face warmed. "A man probably shouldn't see them."

His eyes widened. "*Ach*, okay. I don't think I'd want to read it then."

"I could read some of it to you."

"*Jah*, that might be a better idea. The only woman I want to see is my *fraa*." The side of his mouth twitched.

Ach. Her cheeks warmed. How had they come to *this* conversation? "We should...uh...eat our pretzels."

64

Because if she dwelt on his words too long, her face was sure to catch fire.

Justin chuckled. "That sounds like a *gut* idea."

Ten minutes later, Lucy forsook the second half of her pretzel and knocked on the door of the Silas Miller residence. Justin had said he was going to stop in and say hi to Silas and Paul in their metal shop, so she had several minutes to visit with her friends. Lucy knew Justin was anxious about showing up at her home with her, since her father was the only one who was privy to the situation. It wondered her what *Mamm* would think when she saw the two of them together. Lucy had already invited Justin to take supper with them. It would be an interesting evening, for sure.

She glanced back to see Justin entering the shop, just as the door to the house flew open.

"Lucy! What a happy surprise." Shiloh beamed. "Sierra, Lucy's here!" She called over her shoulder. "*Kumm* in."

Lucy stepped into the house. She heard sounds coming from various areas, and guessed the others were likely playing in their rooms or doing chores.

"I'll go get us a drink and snacks." Shiloh disappeared before Lucy had a chance to decline the offer. She really wasn't hungry after eating the pretzel.

Sierra walked into the living room, wiping her

hands on a dish towel. "Lucy." She smiled and hugged her.

Shiloh joined them and the three of them took a seat on the living room couch.

"Do *not* tell me that was *Justin Beachy* I just saw going into the shop!" Shiloh grinned.

"*What?* Justin 'too hot to handle' Beachy?" Sierra's jaw slacked. "No way. No. Way."

Lucy laughed. She'd forgotten all about the silly name they'd given him. What would Justin think about that?

"Well?" Shiloh bounced.

"*Jah*, it was Justin Beachy," she admitted.

"Lucy Bontrager! You've been holding out on us." Sierra's hand braced her hip.

"So, *that's* where you've been disappearing to after the singings!" Shiloh gasped. "And here I thought you were thinking of jumping the fence or something."

"Never." Lucy asserted, but she didn't correct Shiloh's assumption. It worked to her and Justin's advantage.

Shiloh lowered her voice. "So...does this mean something?"

Lucy's cheeks warmed. "Maybe. We'll have to see."

Shiloh squealed. "*Ach*, I'm so happy for you!"

"I can't believe you've been keeping this from us.

Justin Beachy. Out of all the men." Sierra shook her head. "Oh man, Judah's going to be heartbroken."

"Judah?" Lucy's eyes widened.

"He has had a crush on you for forever. Didn't you ride home with him once?" Shiloh said.

"*Jah*, I did, but..." Lucy shrugged. "I guess there just wasn't a spark. Maybe it was because I knew he was your *bruder*."

"But there's a spark with Justin Beachy." Shiloh's white teeth were nearly blinding. She almost seemed more excited about Lucy and Justin than Lucy was. Almost.

Lucy rubbed her hands on her dress. "*Jah*, there's definitely a spark with Justin."

"You are the luckiest girl alive." Sierra's hands clutched her heart and she practically swooned.

"I know." Lucy sipped her tea and nodded, not able to hide her own grin. "And he's...amazing. Really."

A knock on the door caused Lucy's heart rate to quicken.

"Is that him?" Sierra's eyes flew wide.

"Probably." Lucy shot up from the sofa. "I guess I'd better go."

"I'll get the door, just in case." Shiloh winked before opening the door.

Justin stood in the opening, filling most of it with his masculine presence. Man, he had to be the most handsome man Lucy had ever known.

His warm gaze appraised her. "I just wanted to let you know that I'll be in the buggy. Take as long as you need."

"I'm ready now." Her words tumbled out. While she loved her friends dearly, nothing compared to spending time with Justin.

He nodded, then realized three young women had been staring at him. He silently dismiss himself, then turned around and headed for the buggy.

Sierra giggled. "I think I'm going to give you the nickname Lucky Lucy." She teased. Fortunately, Justin was already out of earshot.

Shiloh pointed at Lucy. "You better be careful. And you know what I mean."

Lucy could feel the heat crawling up her neck. If her friends only knew the truth of the matter.

"*Jah*, he's a Beachy." Sierra nodded. "The last eligible one, unfortunately." She sighed.

Shiloh elbowed her younger *schweschder*.

"Well, I better go. I don't want to keep him waiting." Lucy smiled.

Lucy's friends waved their goodbyes as she and Justin traveled down the Millers' driveway. No doubt, they would be the subject of conversation in the Silas Miller household for the remainder of the evening.

And perhaps many more days thereafter.

NINE

"I'm guessing that went well?" A smile slipped from Justin's lips.

Lucy nodded. "Even better than I'd hoped."

"How so?"

"Shiloh thinks I've been sneaking out with you after the singings. I let her assume it was true."

He nudged her shoulder with his, unable to help a frown forming. "I wish it had been me you'd been sneaking off with."

"*Ach*, Justin. If I had any idea you'd be interested in *me*..." She shook her head.

"Why wouldn't I have been interested in *you*? I mean, besides our age difference and all."

"Well, we were at the same singings." She stared at him. "And you never asked."

He sighed. "Sometimes guys can be clueless. And I'm not that big on social events."

"Which is why you stopped going."

"That and I thought I was getting too old to go. After Joshua and Susan married, it was just awkward to go alone. You know what I mean?" He blew out a long breath.

"Well, this situation would be so much easier. Ha. What am I thinking? I likely wouldn't be in this situation." She groaned. "I'm such a *dummkopp*."

He reached over and squeezed her hand. "Hey, now. Don't beat yourself up about it. It is what it is. You can't go back and change the past, you just have to deal with it the best you can. Learn from your mistakes and move on."

"You're right."

"Besides, I'm glad in a way. I don't know if I would have ever had the pleasure of knowing you otherwise. Because *Gott* knows I probably would have never found the boldness to ask you on a buggy ride. I'd probably end up becoming an old bachelor." When he glanced her way, he noticed her eyes shimmering. "*Ach*, what's wrong?"

"You're so sweet. I don't deserve you." She brushed away a tear with a shaky hand.

"I am nothing."

"*Ach*, Justin Beachy. You are more than you'll ever know. I've only known you a few hours and you've already captured my heart."

He reached over and grasped her hand. "Likewise."

"How are you not married?"

He shrugged. "I guess *Der Herr* was saving me for you." He reached over and slipped his arm around her and they rode in silence for several minutes with nothing but the horse's clip clops and buggy wheels turning. He felt her body relax against him. He loved the feel of her leaning into him.

The closer they inched toward the Bontrager residence, the more nervous Justin became, though. He'd only been there a handful of times for Sunday meeting. How would Lucy's family react to his presence? "Who do you think will be there?"

"Probably *Dat*, *Mamm*, Linda, and Marcus."

"Your *bruder* and *schweschder*?"

"*Jah*. Do you know them?" She glanced at him.

"*Nee*."

"Are you nervous?" She moved slightly and he brought his hand back to the reins.

"A little."

She blew out a long breath. "Me too. I just don't want to have to lie."

"You don't have to. Just be vague."

"What do you mean?"

"Well, if someone asks how long we've been

seeing each other, I plan to say a little while." He shrugged. "They can determine what that is in their own mind."

Lucy tilted her head.

"Another option is to just say it's none of their business. Of course, you wouldn't want to say that to your *mamm*." Justin chuckled.

"*Nee*. She wouldn't like that." She nibbled her fingernail. "What if she asks me if I'm in the *familye* way?"

"Tell her the truth. She will likely assume I'm the father since we'll be there together. And because I carry the Beachy name, of course." He shook his head. "You know, the Beachys really do have a much better reputation in Pennsylvania."

"Your *brieder's* behavior is not your fault, you know." Lucy's forehead wrinkled, then he noticed she became teary-eyed again. "I don't...I'm sorry I'm ruining your reputation too. You're a *gut* guy and you deserve much better than me."

"*Ach*, I didn't mean that."

Her chin quivered. "You can still back out of this, if you want to. No one would blame you. Especially not me."

He slowed his driving horse and brought the buggy to a stop on the side of the quiet gravel road they'd been on for the last few minutes. "Hey, now. *Kumm* here." He beckoned her close with his hand.

She leaned toward him, and he brought her head to his chest, wrapping her in his arms. He didn't say anything but allowed her to cry for a minute. If her hair had been down, he imagined he'd be softly combing his fingers through it.

"I'm sorry. I shouldn't have said anything. Honestly, I don't mind. I like us together." He rubbed her back. "And I like you in my arms," he murmured and pressed his lips to the side of her traveling bonnet. She likely didn't feel a thing.

She pulled back and stared at him. Her eyes searched his. "Do you mean that?"

"Wouldn't have said it if I didn't." He smiled and thumbed away her remaining tears.

"*Denki.*"

"I meant it when I said you've captured my heart." He squeezed her hand. "Should we continue to your folks' place now?"

"*Jah.*"

"Are you sure? Because we could stay just like this for a few more hours and I'd be satisfied." He couldn't contain his smile because he meant every word. Who knew a *maedel* could make him this *ferhoodled*? He surely would have never imagined it.

"I'd love to. But we should probably get this visit over with, ain't so?"

He chuckled. "*Jah*, you're right."

~

Lucy didn't know who was more nervous, her or Justin. As they pulled into their driveway, she directed Justin to the hitching post just outside the barn, where he could tether the horse. Although, if he ended up staying long, it might be better to put the mare in a paddock.

"It looks like *Dat* is in the barn. You could go say hello to him."

"Just me?" His brow arched.

"*Jah*, that way I can answer any questions *Mamm* and Linda might have. And it'll be less awkward for you if you walk in with *Dat*, I think." She lifted her chin toward the barn. "My *bruder* could be in there too."

"That's *gut* to know. I wouldn't want to say anything I shouldn't."

"Wish me luck." She shifted to descend from the buggy.

"I'll do one better. I'll pray." He hopped down and hurried to her side. "Wait. Let me help."

She took his hand as he assisted her exit. "*Denki.*"

His hand lingered on hers, then he brushed the top of it with his thumb before reluctantly letting go. It might have been a small gesture, but it was enough to stir her heart. Was he oblivious to the sparks he was igniting, or did he feel them too? It had been heavenly when he'd held her in his arms earlier. She could have stayed that way all night.

Her eyes studied his. "You'll never know how much I appreciate you."

His mouth opened slightly but snapped shut when her father approached.

"Lucy, I think your mother and *schweschder* could use some help with supper," *Dat* said.

Lucy took that as her cue to get scarce. She shared one more longing glance with Justin, then headed toward the house. Before stepping into her home, she caught *Dat* and Justin walking out toward the field. No doubt Justin was filling *Dat* in on their goings-on today. Would they be speaking of a wedding date too?

Oh, she hoped so.

TEN

"I didn't expect you'd stay at Justin Beachy's all day, *dochder*." *Mamm* eyed Lucy with suspicion. "Is there something going on that I should be aware of?"

"We're dating." She admitted, then turned at her *schweschder's* sharp gasp.

"*You're* dating Justin Beachy?" Linda's eyes bugged.

Mamm's head shook. "I should have known. *Kumm, dochder.*" *Mamm* led the way to her room, then closed the two of them inside. No doubt her *schweschder* was eavesdropping on the other side of the door.

Ach. Lucy suddenly felt queasy. Was it the *boppli* or nerves?

Mamm pulled out the pregnancy book Lucy had hidden under her mattress. "I found this today.

Would you mind explaining what you were doing with it?"

Lucy hung her head but didn't answer.

"Tell me the truth. Are you in the *familye* way, *dochder*?"

"Oh, *Mamm*!" She burst into tears.

Mamm's hand planted on her hip. "What were you thinking, dating a Beachy? And one that's quite a bit older—and no doubt more *experienced*—than you."

Poor Justin. "Justin's a *gut* man, *Mamm*. And I don't care if he's older."

Mamm snorted. "*Nee. Gut* men don't do this sort of thing, Lucy. You should have known better."

Lucy hated the fact that Justin was being blamed for *her* indiscretion, but she kept her mouth closed.

"Do you realize how this is going to make your father look?" *Mamm* shook her head. "I can just hear people now. *He shouldn't be bishop if he can't even keep control over his own household.*"

There was so much Lucy wanted to say, but she'd learned at a young age when to keep her thoughts to herself. This was one of those times.

"I'm guessing this means there will be a wedding soon?"

Lucy nodded. She sent a quick prayer Heavenward for Justin's willingness to step in. He was the most unselfish person she'd ever met.

"Is that what Justin Beachy and your *Dat* are talking about right now?"

"Probably."

"Well, I guess it is what it is, then." *Mamm* sighed, then handed the pregnancy book to Lucy. "Go ahead and take this. You're going to need it."

"*Denki, Mamm.*" She'd stuff it into her bag upstairs and take it with her next time she went to Justin's, which she suspected would be tomorrow.

"Put that away and help your *schweschder* set the table now." *Mamm* said prior to slipping out of the room.

Lucy took a deep breath, wiped the wetness from her face, then straightened her dress. She hadn't expected a hug or any type of affection. That wasn't their way. Truth be told, it hadn't gone as bad with *Mamm* or *Dat* as she thought it would.

"*Denki, Gott.*" She breathed out the nearly inaudible words.

~

"By the looks your mother was giving me at supper, I'm guessing she knows?" Justin's brow arched as they strolled toward the barn.

"*Jah.*" Lucy glanced back to make sure they weren't being followed. She lowered her voice. "*Mamm* found the pregnancy book in my room and asked me about it. I had already told her that you and I were dating, so she assumed the *boppli* was yours."

"That explains why she was frowning at me like I was the devil." He shrugged. "Oh, well. I guess I better get used to it."

"I'm so sorry. I—"

He stopped walking and held up a hand. "No more apologizing." He lifted her chin so she couldn't help but look into his eyes. "Okay?"

She nodded and they resumed their journey. "What did you and *Dat* talk about before supper?"

"The wedding, mostly. He said that he'd talk to the leaders this week and get back to us."

She nibbled her fingernail.

"You know, if you're wanting me to kiss you, you might want to ditch that habit."

"*Ach.*" She yanked her finger from her mouth. If Justin Beachy intended to kiss her, she'd never put her finger to her mouth again.

He chuckled. "I was teasing you. If I had in mind to kiss you, I reckon there'd be *very* little that could stop me."

They rounded the corner of the barn, now out of view of anyone who might be watching from the house.

She swallowed. Did he plan to kiss her tonight before he left? *Ach*, if only it were so.

"Did you have a *gut* time today?" he asked.

"I did."

His smile reached his eyes, crinkling the skin at the corners. "Me too."

"Do you think we make a *gut* match?"

"I do. Do you?" His voice dipped. *Ach*, he had the most amazing voice.

She nodded and smiled. "The best."

"I know we just officially met today, but I feel like I already know you. Is that even possible?"

"I think so." She tapped her lips, then remembered his comment about kissing. "It's funny how much your life can change in just a day, ain't so?"

"It is." He stopped walking and stared into her eyes.

"I was so nervous about meeting you this morning."

"If it makes you feel better, I was nervous too." His fingers brushed her forearm. "And I honestly hate the fact that I have to say goodbye to you tonight. I wish..." His voice trailed off.

Her breath hitched as he took a step toward her. Was it possible that Justin Beachy was falling in love with her?

The squeak from the screen door distracted them.

"*Ach*, I should probably go and let you get some sleep," he said.

Lucy took a small step backward and found herself against the barn. Justin's left arm pressed the metal wall beside her. His chest rose and fell, and desire burned in his eyes. Her heart pounded even more as his right hand moved to cradle her face. His thumb slowly roamed over her cheek in a gentle caress, then he dipped his head to brush his lips against her forehead.

"*Guten nacht, schatzi,*" his hoarse voice whispered.

Then she watched, dumbfounded, as he abruptly turned and headed toward his buggy.

As he drove down the driveway, he lifted his hand in a small wave. She stared until he drove out of sight, then allowed herself to swoon.

Nee, it hadn't been a lip kiss, but it had been every bit as romantic and amazing and *wunderbaar* as one.

She was certain she'd never forget it for as long as she lived.

How Justin Beachy had managed to stay single for so long, she'd never understand. He was a treasure, indeed.

~

Two hours after Justin had left, Lucy found herself wide awake lying in her dark bedroom. Shadows from the tree branches rustling in the wind danced on her walls. Everyone else had long been asleep.

Her hand rested on her abdomen, and she thought about the *boppli's* father. Where was Trey right now and what was he doing? Was he safe? Was he in the middle of a battle on the other side of the world? Was he still alive? Would he ever know about his child?

Was she betraying Justin by having these thoughts?

Nee. She didn't think so. She couldn't help but wonder about these things.

Even if Trey were to come to her house tonight, tell her that he loved her, offer to join the Amish and marry her, she would decline his offer. Because, while she'd thought that she loved Trey, she realized how superficial their love had been.

Trey was a great guy. He was funny, nice, fun, and he was a *gut* kisser, if she admitted it to herself. But most of their relationship had been built on excitement and infatuation. There was a world of difference between her relationship with Trey and her courtship with Justin.

Justin hadn't asked anything of her but sacrificed his own reputation. Not only that, but he'd also given up his time, his freedom, and basically the whole rest of his life just to make an honest woman out of her. Not that what they were doing was honest. And that was another thing. He was essentially lying, and likely going against his own conscience, to protect her and spare her from shame.

What kind of a man did that? What kind of a person would give up *everything* for a practical stranger?

Aside from what Jesus had done when He went to the cross, she'd never seen that kind of selfless love. And the more she pondered their situation, the more she realized that Justin Beachy was truly one of a kind.

ELEVEN

$\mathcal{J}$ustin tapped his leg, waiting on the porch for his driver to show up. Saturday morning was the day Justin met for men's fellowship with his *brieder*, Sammy, and some of the other guys in the two neighboring communities. Although he was looking forward to it, he was nervous.

Today, he'd divulge his plans to marry Lucy. The news was certain to be met with hesitancy and possibly discouragement from some, but he'd already mentally prepared himself. Having Sammy on his side was a great comfort.

Last time he'd spoken with Lucy's father, he'd said the leaders would stop by Justin's home tonight. Which meant he'd probably receive a reprimand and be assigned a wedding date. To say he was anxious would be an understatement.

After spending the last few days and a night with

Lucy, he was ready to begin the rest of his life with her.

They'd shared so many things; their favorite colors—they both shared a love of green; their favorite foods—his was barbequed ribs and hers was spaghetti; their favorite animals—he liked horses and she liked squirrels. Squirrels! Of all things. He hadn't told her that he used to hunt them with his *brieder*.

They both enjoyed all kinds of games, and the two of them assembled a puzzle the day she'd spent all night at his place. They discussed favorite Bible verses and songs—just about anything they could think of. He truly felt they had formed a solid friendship, if not more.

And their first kiss? *Ach*, their first kiss had been amazing. He could recall it vividly.

Lucy had been in his kitchen, rustling up ingredients to prepare supper for the two of them, when he'd walked in with a wrapped box.

"What is that?" Lucy's smile could've hung the moon.

He'd shrugged. "A little something I picked up for you. Open it." He urged.

She pulled the ribbon off, then tore the wrapping paper, her smile not leaving her face. When she opened the box and pulled out the gift, she giggled at the "Kiss the cook" message on the apron he'd chosen. It had been absolutely perfect.

"Should I help you put it on?" He offered.

She nodded.

He took his time tying the strings behind her neck and around her waist, lingering on purpose. Then he stepped back. "There you go."

"I love it."

"Me too."

She stared at him, fighting a smile. "Well?"

He took a step closer. "Well, what?" he murmured, leaning close to her ear. He loved teasing her.

Instead of waiting for him, she'd hooked her fingers around one of his suspenders, wrapped her other hand around his neck, and brought his lips down on hers. From there, he took over and pulled her into his arms. His mouth blissfully moved over hers, then momentarily left to explore her delicate jawline and neck. His hands ached to explore as well, but he forbade them to do so. His lips returned to hers and he deepened the kiss. Her heart beating against his chest sparked a desire that coursed through his entire being. When he could hardly stand it, he forced himself back.

"Ach, it's so easy to get carried away." He finally caught his breath.

"I can't wait to get carried away with you," she murmured, her cheeks flushed.

His fingers caressed her earlobe. "Soon, lieb. Very

soon." He indulged in one more brief kiss before commanding himself to refrain.

Lucy grasped his hand, her eyes searching his. "I love you, Justin Beachy."

The passenger van pulled up, ruining his lovely daydream. *Jah,* their wedding couldn't come soon enough as far as he was concerned. He'd managed to behave himself, even when she'd spent the night, although it hadn't been easy. Today would be the only day this week that he wouldn't spend with her, but he'd hoped to visit after the leaders left this evening. Even so, he'd be missing her.

~

Fellowship with the men had been *wunderbaar* as always. Time with his brothers in Christ always lifted Justin's spirits. As usual, Sammy's Scripture readings had been on point. The verses he'd read today centered around fleeing temptation and allowing God's Spirit to lead them. A couple of verses had jumped out at Justin specifically. *But put ye on the Lord Jesus Christ, and make not provision for the flesh, to fulfill the lusts thereof.* And also, *Walk in the Spirit, and ye shall not fulfill the lust of the flesh.*

Jah, walking in the Spirit and putting on the Lord Jesus Christ was certainly something he needed to do more of. Because spending time alone with Lucy bred more temptation than he cared to admit. He knew it was a temptation for her too. The last thing he wanted to do was cause Lucy to sin.

Sammy cleared his throat. "Justin has something he'd like to share with everyone."

Justin took a deep breath and released it. This was it.

"I thought y'all should be the first to know. I'm getting married." Justin smiled at the thought of taking Lucy as his *fraa*.

"You're *what*?" His *bruder* Jaden rocked back in his chair a little too far, sending it sliding out from under him.

The other guys chuckled, and Sammy offered Jaden a hand up off the floor.

"I didn't even realize you were dating anyone." His older *bruder* Josiah scratched his beard.

"*Jah*, Lucy Bontrager," Justin admitted.

"*Lucy Bontrager?* You don't mean the bishop's youngest *dochder*?" It was Paul Miller this time.

"*Jah*, he sure does," Nathaniel, the youngest Miller brother, said. "Saw the two of them together. They're definitely...*involved*." Nathaniel raised a judgmental brow. According to Justin's brothers Jaden and Joshua, Nathaniel had never been much of a Beachy fan.

"I forgot to mention that Justin stopped by the shop the other day when you were out, Paul," Silas Miller said. "Justin and Lucy were all the *maed* talked about that night." He chuckled.

Gut, so they *had* been believable. He'd have to tell Lucy.

"How come you're planning on getting married, and we're *just* finding out you've been dating? *Wait*." Jaden held out his hand. "You're not...she's not..."

Justin frowned at his *bruder* with a warning attached, and his eyes begged Sammy for help. *Ach*, he really didn't want to have to explain himself in front of everyone.

"Let's not accuse anyone of anything," Sammy said.

"Innocent till proven guilty. Even so, it's none of our business," Silas Miller chimed in.

"Right. *We* have no right to say anything, Jaden," Josiah said.

Michael Eicher held up both hands. "I know I don't."

Nathaniel's mouth opened. "Wait. Are you saying—?"

Sammy held up a hand. "He isn't saying *anything* except that he is gettin' hitched. Besides, like Silas said, it's none of our business." Sammy tossed Nathaniel a reproving look.

"I didn't know you and Lucy were dating, either. I'm sure Susan would have said something," his youngest *bruder* Joshua remarked.

"Only a few people know. We haven't said anything to anyone *on purpose*." Justin's gaze slid to Nathaniel.

"Well, your secret's safe with us," Sammy said, then examined each of the other men in the room. "Right, guys?"

"Is it a secret?" Timothy Stoltzfoos spoke up.

"Just until the *banns* are published," Justin said.

"And when will that be?" Joshua asked.

"Not sure yet. Next Sunday, probably." Justin didn't make eye contact with anyone because he knew their mouths were probably agape. He was sure and certain his *brieder* must have a few questions right about then. "I'm not getting any younger."

"Congratulations." Titus Troyer, who'd kept silent, offered his hand.

Justin smiled and shook it. "*Denki*."

"Me and Emily are a *gut* number of years apart too." Titus grinned. "It's not really a big deal."

Justin appreciated Titus's words.

~

"It looks like the driver's here." Timothy remarked.

Justin, Joshua, Paul, Silas, Timothy, Nathaniel,

and Titus all rode over to the neighboring district together. Sammy, Michael, and Justin's older *brieder*, Josiah and Jaden, all lived there in Detweiler's stricter Amish district. Justin had heard that Sammy had been reprimanded on more than one occasion for hosting their inter-district men's Bible study group. But one thing Justin knew about Sammy was that if he knew something was *Gott's* will, he wasn't going to let the leadership—or anyone—stop him.

"We ought to obey *Gott*, rather than men." Justin had heard Sammy assert.

"Hey, Justin, wait up," Jaden called as he headed toward the van.

Justin stopped and watched as the other men entered the waiting vehicle. "*Jah*?"

His *bruder* leaned close and whispered, "Is she in the *familye* way?"

Ach. Justin grimaced and stared at his *bruder* but didn't offer an answer or an explanation. He guessed Jaden received confirmation in his silence.

"Justin. How long have you two been seeing each other?" Jaden's countenance was riddled with sympathy. *Jah*, his *bruder* would understand. He'd been through his own battles.

"Long enough," Justin replied, then continued toward the vehicle. He stopped and turned before entering. When he caught Jaden's eye, he made a gesture zipping his lips.

His *bruder* nodded and waved goodbye.

Justin hoped Jaden wouldn't share the news with his *fraa*, because if he did, the entire district would likely know prior to the wedding. If Nathaniel's *fraa* didn't let the cat out of the bag first. Because Justin was certain that Nathaniel would share the news with his family.

And news of a sudden wedding would surely set the rumor mill on fire.

TWELVE

*J*ustin had been pacing the floor more over the last week than in his entire life prior. Of course, he'd never had so much to be concerned over. His life had turned completely upside down. He had a difficult time recognizing himself these days.

Being a bachelor evoked *so* much less drama.

Would he miss the quiet calm he'd felt up until this week? Or would things settle down once he and Lucy were hitched? He surely hoped so. Because now that he'd met and fallen in love with Lucy, he couldn't imagine doing life without her. He'd be downright lonely. If he had to choose a quiet life alone or a hectic one with Lucy, he'd choose her. Every time.

Now, if he could have her *and* a quiet life, he reckoned life would be close to perfect.

After he'd returned from his men's group, he stopped by Millers' and picked up some fresh cinnamon rolls to serve the guests he was expecting. Maybe they'd be less harsh if they were eating something sweet and delicious? One could only hope.

It wondered him how Jerry would act among them. Would he be playing the part of bishop keeping a rigid stance? Or perhaps, since it was his *dochder* who was involved in the transgression, he'd be lenient amongst his peers.

All Justin knew was that he hoped they didn't require a kneeling confession in front of the church. Because if they did, Justin would be required to lie about sinning with Lucy. And who in their right mind would kneel before the holy *Gott* of the universe and confess to a sin that they didn't commit? That would be like lying directly to *Der Herr*. It was something he wasn't willing to do.

A few hours later, he was serving his guests cinnamon rolls and coffee. They'd all settled around the dining table. Justin had insisted the bishop take the head seat, then took his place after everyone else was seated. Jerry had motioned for Justin to sit next to him.

It was times like this that he was thankful he'd spent the extra money and purchased the large table when he'd moved into this house in his new district. Every Amish family he knew of had a large or extra-large dining set. But at the time, he couldn't see beyond himself sitting at this table all alone, save for the rare occasions his family members might visit. But now, this table and the previously empty chairs sparked excitement in his soul. How many years would it take before they were all filled with his own *kinner*? It had been something he'd never been able to imagine. But now? Now, it held a world of possibilities.

"Let's pray," the bishop said, distracting Justin from his thoughts. Each one bowed his head while Jerry uttered a silent prayer. Jerry looked to the other leaders. "Thank you all for joining me today to address this very serious matter."

The other leaders nodded.

Justin folded his hands, then unfolded them and wiped them on his pants, then folded them again. *Jah*, he was nervous.

"Justin Beachy, is it true that you've been courting my *dochder* Lucy Bontrager?" Jerry looked him straight in the eye. Something in his mien told Justin he could trust him to lead the meeting in an appropriate way.

"*Jah*." Justin agreed to what they both already knew was true. He guessed the bishop said what he did for the sake of the other leaders present.

"And is it also true that Lucy is in the *familye* way?" Jerry couldn't hide his disappointment. No doubt, his *dochder's* behavior had been a grief to him. Or perhaps Jerry counted the transgression a failure of his own somehow.

"*Jah*, it's true." Justin hung his head and silently thanked *Der Herr* for Jerry's wisdom. *Nee*, it wasn't right to deceive the other leaders, but nothing Justin had agreed to was untrue.

"Since you have confessed this before the leaders, we have agreed that a public confession won't be necessary." The bishop looked amongst the other men. "With that being the case, we have also agreed that the two of you should marry as soon as possible. Because of the nature of the sin, you will not be allowed to have a formal wedding. You will marry during the next meeting."

His chest thumped hard. *The next meeting? Ach*, he hadn't been expecting it to be *that* soon.

"*Denki* for your grace." Justin nodded to the men.

"It is the grace of *Gott* that cleanses from all sin," the minister added.

Jerry looked to the other leaders. "Do you have anything to add?"

The deacon, who was also his neighbor Nathaniel's father-in-law, spoke up. "I think it might be a *gut* idea for the two of you to abstain from contact until the wedding."

Ach. An entire week without seeing Lucy?

"They will need to confer on wedding preparations." The minister set his cinnamon roll on his plate. "How about they refrain from seeing each other till Friday? I think that will give them enough time to prepare."

Justin could kiss the minister. But what on earth would he do with himself all week? There went his plans for the evening. He'd have to ask Jerry to apologize to Lucy for him.

After they'd polished off their cinnamon rolls and coffee, the men headed out together. All the men, except for Jerry, had come in one buggy. He lingered a few extra moments after the men headed down the driveway.

"I am greatly indebted to you, Justin Beachy." Jerry shook his hand.

"I'm beginning to think it's the other way around. I've fallen in love with your *dochder*."

The bishop's eyes widened. "You have?"

"I'm going to miss her something wonderful next week. Will you—?" Justin pivoted and headed to the kitchen. He grabbed a notepad from the drawer and jotted a message on it, then bagged up one of the cinnamon rolls and handed them both to Jerry. "Will you give this to Lucy, please?"

"I will." Tenderness flickered across Bishop Jerry's face. It was plain to see he loved his *dochder*. Justin hadn't really thought much beyond the wedding, but he realized in that moment that having Jerry Bontrager as his father-in-law would be a true blessing.

Justin accompanied the bishop as he strolled out to his buggy.

Jerry rubbed his beard. "If you happened to show up at the library in town, say around ten on Tuesday morning, to check out a book or something..." A sly smile formed on the bishop's face and he shrugged.

"*Ach, jah*. I don't think the leaders would have a problem with me checking out a book." His grin widened.

Jerry picked up the leather reins. "Welp. It's about that time. I expect I'll be seeing you on Friday, then?"

"Lord willing."

THIRTEEN

*L*ucy stepped into the library and immediately inhaled. *Ach*, she'd always loved the smell of books. Perhaps Justin would build her a few bookshelves for their home. That would be *wunderbaar*. As it was, the small bookcase she had in her bedroom could hardly contain her collection. Did Justin like to read too? That had been one thing they hadn't discussed yet.

She knew exactly which section she wanted to explore today: Pregnancy and Marriage. She needed tips on both. If she could accomplish a healthy pregnancy and a happy husband, she was pretty sure she could accomplish anything.

"Lucy?"

She slid the book back into its place on the shelf and turned at the male voice.

"Trey?" Her eyes widened at his approach. "What

are you doing here? I thought you were out of the country." Trey was the last person she expected to see at the library, but there he was, the biological father of her *boppli*, in the flesh.

"It's great to see you too, babe." He wiggled his eyebrows. "Unfortunately, I was wounded during a training exercise, and they sent me home to recover. I had surgery a couple weeks ago, but I'm healing up pretty good. I'll be back on my game soon. I've been bored out of my mind, which is why I'm here. I'm glad I ran into you."

Before she knew it, he'd grasped her hand and swooped in and stole a kiss on the cheek. She stepped back and gasped. It was a *gut* thing they were back in the corner out of view and hopefully earshot of other patrons. If anyone from the *g'may* were to see them here together, it would prove disastrous.

His head cocked to the side. "What's the problem? You've never shied away from a kiss before."

"We're not together anymore, remember?" She frowned.

"We can still be friends, right? Why don't we meet up for dinner one of these days? We can hang out at my place afterward." His smoldering gaze hinted he had more than dinner and hanging out in mind.

"No, I can't."

He glanced around them, examining the titles on

the shelf. "What are you...? Are you looking at pregnancy books?" His mouth gaped and he stared in confusion at her flat middle section.

~

"*Ach*, there you are." Justin stepped around a bookshelf, moved beside Lucy, and slipped his arm around her waist. It wasn't their way to show affection in public, but he thought it was necessary, considering the circumstances. He hadn't meant to be eavesdropping, but when he'd heard Lucy's voice in conjunction with a male voice, he'd paused, waiting for the right moment to show himself.

"Justin?" Lucy's pleased expression widened. Had her father not informed her that he'd be there? "I didn't expect to see you."

The young man, whom he assumed was Trey, stared at him. His confused gaze bounced back and forth between Justin and Lucy.

Lucy recovered from her surprise. She turned to Trey. "This is my fiancé, Justin Beachy."

Justin smiled down at her and relief flooded her mien.

Trey frowned. "Wait. You're engaged to an Amish guy? Seriously?"

"*Jah,* she is." Justin nodded.

"I thought..." Trey's eyes shot from her flat abdomen to the bookshelf in front of them, then lifted to Justin. He huffed. "Never mind. So, what? Were you cheating on me? Or on both of us?"

"Uh..." Lucy's eyes pled for help.

Justin frowned. "Who are you?" He figured it was the *boppli's* father, but he needed to ask anyhow, to change the subject, if for nothing else.

"I *was* her boyfriend." He scowled at Lucy.

"Well, you're not anymore. She's getting married to me on Sunday," Justin asserted.

"Seriously, Lucy?" He stared at her, and for a moment, Justin thought he'd detected disappointment flicker across his face. "I can't believe this."

Lucy nodded, squeezing Justin's hand.

"Fine then. I guess we're over." Trey shrugged as though it were no big deal, but Justin understood the hurt and anger in his expression. He truly felt sorry for the guy. He was losing Lucy to another man, after all.

As soon as Trey walked off, Lucy fell into Justin's arms. "*Denki.*" She released a sniffle. "I didn't know what to say or do."

He pulled back. "Your father didn't tell you I was coming to the library?"

"*Nee.* Now I know why he suggested I come here." She smiled now.

"We can't be seen together by anyone in the *g'may*." He glanced around, thankful for their seclusion.

"*Jah*, I know." She reached up and touched his cheek. "I've missed you."

"I missed you too." He glanced toward the end of the bookcase. "So that was Trey, huh?"

She frowned. "*Jah*."

"Well, I don't think he'll be coming around again, since he knows you're getting hitched."

"*Nee*, he won't."

He held her at arm's length and stared into her eyes. "I love you. You know that, right?"

She nodded.

His finger trailed her cheek. "I wish we'd met before you and Trey got involved."

"I know. Me too." Her hands twisted. "I'd always hoped you'd ask me home from a singing."

"And I didn't even think twice because I thought you were too young. Apparently, I was wrong." He sighed. "Unfortunately, there's nothing we can do to change the past."

"Maybe there's a reason for all this. Maybe *Der Herr* wanted this *boppli* to be born. Maybe He has something planned for her."

His brow lifted. "Her?"

Her smile widened. "I have a feeling."

FOURTEEN

*E*arlier in the week, Justin had made a trip out to Titus and Emily Troyer's place to see about Titus crafting a special wedding gift for Lucy. He had a talent for woodworking, and Justin had been impressed by some of the items Titus had shown him in the past.

Justin already had in mind to hire Titus to craft a cradle for the *boppli* once Lucy's time got closer, but he wanted something special as a wedding gift. Something personal. Something big. He had no clue what, though, so he'd asked Titus for ideas.

His friend had suggested a few different things, and they all sounded great to Justin. But Titus only had a week to complete the project, so Justin chose something simple but intimate. He couldn't wait to see it once it was completed.

While Justin was there, he observed their precious

family. An irrepressible desire filled his heart, and he suddenly couldn't wait to hold his and Lucy's *boppli* in his arms. Of course, the *boppli* wasn't his biologically, but he knew he would love and care for it—*nee, her*—just the same. He was certain becoming a *dat* would be natural to him. He'd always loved *kinner*.

Now, to get through their wedding.

~

Lucy had chosen a special green fabric for her wedding dress, since she and Justin shared a fondness for the color. She guessed he was probably expecting her to wear a blue hue, since that was more common in his former Amish district in Pennsylvania. They hadn't discussed her dress and she hoped he wouldn't bring it up when he stopped by today, because she wanted it to be a surprise.

She'd loved sewing it and the white apron she'd wear with it. She couldn't help but imagine their wedding day. *Nee*, it wouldn't be a fancy ordeal with several hundred guests. It would simply be their *g'may* and a few other friends and family members from the neighboring district.

Justin and her family would be transforming their barn into a reception area. The church and the wedding ceremony would be held down the road at the Henry Troyer residence. Their district owned two church wagons for special occasions, such as this. Since the extra wagon stayed at the bishop's house when it wasn't needed, they'd be able to prepare without disrupting preparations for Sunday's church service. *Dat* planned to make an announcement for the reception after their vows were spoken during church.

Lucy already had in mind to ask Shiloh and Sierra to be her impromptu side sitters. They wouldn't have special-made dresses, but they'd be wearing their Sunday best. Now that she thought of it, she could sew each of them a new white apron. *Jah*, she'd have enough time to do that. She only wished she could give them each a little something special to remember the day by. She'd been to many weddings over the last few years, and the bride and groom always provided a personalized gift for their attendants. Maybe she'd ask Justin for ideas.

Lucy didn't know if Justin had anyone in mind to ask to be his attendants. Since his *brieder* and most of his friends his age were already married, he'd likely choose someone younger. Maybe Shiloh and Sierra would have some ideas. After all, they would be the ones accompanying the young men throughout the event.

As soon as she heard Justin's carriage traveling up the driveway, she squealed and hurried out to meet him. To her surprise, he'd brought several helpers with him. *Dat* would be grateful that Justin's brothers Joshua, Jaden, and Josiah had all come along.

Jah, she was certain the Beachy brothers could be on the covers of those magazines at Walmart.

Only one of them stirred her heart, though. Justin's long legs striding toward her proved that fact. She moved toward him, closing the gap between them. *Ach*, if only they could steal away for a kiss or two.

"How are you feeling?" He briefly brushed her hand with his, but abstained from further contact.

Did he have any idea that his slightest touch, the timbre of his voice, his masculine scent, sent her heart galloping into next Tuesday? *Ach*, their wedding couldn't come soon enough.

"*Gut.*" Her hand instinctively moved to her abdomen.

"No sickness?" He'd seen the effects of pregnancy the couple of the days she'd spent at his house. On one of their excursions, he'd had to stop the buggy and let her out. She was fine when she remembered to drink her ginger tea, though.

"A little yesterday."

"I'll have to stock up on that tea your *mamm* buys."

Just the thought of his caring ways prompted tears. What kind of man would ruin his reputation, take in a virtual stranger *for life*, and agree to raise a *boppli* that was not his own? Justin Beachy was beyond any dream she could ever conjure up.

"Hormones?" He fetched a handkerchief out of his pocket and handed it to her.

She wiped her tears with his hanky and smiled. "*Jah.*"

"Want to say hello to my brothers?" He reached for her hand.

"Sure."

Within a couple of hours, they had everything set up and ready for their big day. Everyone had headed into the house for a snack, but Justin and Lucy lingered in the barn.

Justin took her hand in his as they stood in front of their special wedding table, the *Eck*, in the corner. "Can you believe we'll be sitting here in just a couple of days, celebrating our marriage?"

Ach, did she see tears shimmering in his eyes?

She stared up at him in amazement. How was it possible that a man of such great character would choose her?

Justin drew her into his arms. "I'm so glad *Der Herr* chose you for me, Lucy Bontrager."

Jah, it had to be *Der Herr,* she agreed. There was no other explanation.

At his last words, he lowered his head and bestowed the most beautiful kiss she'd ever experienced. *Jah*, she was certain being married to this man would be like one of those fairytale books she'd read when she was young. Because he definitely treated her like his princess.

FIFTEEN

Justin figured their wedding day was every bit as exciting, and just as nerve wracking, as it would have been if they'd married during a normal wedding day. Part of him was relieved they didn't have to stand before many hundreds of witnesses, some of whom they wouldn't have known. He was glad for the intimacy that being surrounded by close friends and family afforded.

The preaching had seemed to take forever, and he'd been so lost in his own thoughts he wasn't sure he'd heard most of the sermons. He'd guess that was typical for a bridegroom. How could one focus when they were standing on the precipice of "till death do us part"?

Gott, *I'm doing the right thing, right?*

When Bishop Bontrager called him and Lucy forward, Justin froze. Instead of rising from his bench, he stared up at Lucy and the bishop. Lucy's brow furrowed and she frowned. The bishop moved his head ever so slightly, motioning for him to join them. But he couldn't move, and he was unsure why.

The bishop approached and leaned down to his ear. "Do you still want to marry *mei dochder*?"

His eyes found Lucy's, where tears shimmered. He looked up at the bishop. "*Jah*, I do."

The bishop expelled a sigh of relief. "*Kumm* then."

"I can't move." He frowned.

The bishop summoned Lucy over. "Help me get him up," he whispered.

"Justin, what's wrong?" Her voice was soft.

He grimaced.

The bishop gestured for Lucy to grasp his arm, and he took Justin's other one. "It's just cold feet, *jah*? Happens to the best of us. Do you think you can stand?"

"*Nee*, not yet." He stared at the bishop. "May I have a minute to speak with Lucy?"

Jerry's eyes widened. "Now?"

Justin nodded.

"*Ach*, okay. I will stall for you." The bishop stood before the congregation, indicating that it would be a few moments, then preceded to lead the congregation in song.

Lucy sat next to him and took his hand in hers. "Tell me what's wrong." She spoke in a hushed tone, although those around them wouldn't be able to hear over the singing anyway.

He stared at her, hating the doubt he was feeling. Hating the fear surrounding his heart. Hating that his next words might hurt Lucy. "Are you *sure* you can remain faithful to our marriage?"

Her chin trembled. *Jah*, he'd hurt her. "Justin...you don't trust me?" She wiped away a tear. "I wouldn't be standing here if I wasn't ready to commit to *you*. For life. I love you more than just about anything, Justin Beachy. Do you not feel the same about me?"

"I do." He shook his head. "I'm sorry."

"You are nervous, ain't so?"

"*Jah*."

She squeezed his hand. "It's almost over. Just a few more minutes and it will be done."

He nodded.

"We can do this."

He attempted a reassuring smile.

Several moments later, they stood before the *g'may*, pledging their lives and their love to each other. Justin had finally come to terms with reality. Even if his *fraa* left him in the future, he would survive. Even if the *boppli's* father came and took her away, he would survive. Even if all his worst nightmares were realized, he would survive.

It would only be by the grace of God, but he would survive. Because God was all he truly needed.

~

The reception following the wedding had been everything Lucy hoped it would be. Shiloh and Sierra had been thrilled, the day before, when she'd presented them with their aprons and an invitation to join Lucy and Justin at the *Eck*. Shiloh suggested Mikey Eicher as one of the side sitters for Justin, and he'd liked the idea. It made Lucy wonder if maybe Shiloh had a crush on Mikey. Justin's other attendant was Lucy's older *bruder*, whom Sierra knew as a friend. Both friends seemed satisfied with Justin's choices.

The food, the games, the laughter...everything had been wonderful. But as wonderful as everything had gone, a single thought niggled in the back of Lucy's mind. Was her husband all right?

SIXTEEN

Being married to Lucy was a *wunderbaar* dream, Justin decided. He hadn't known what he'd been missing out on until he met her. He made sure to thank *Der Herr* for her every day. He hoped he would always see her for what she was—a gift straight from *Gott*, something to be cherished.

Although he figured some people in the *g'may* viewed him as less than proper, he found his comfort in knowing the truth of the matter. Fortunately, he knew nobody would ever say anything to his face. And if anyone ever did, he wouldn't care. He'd do it all over again to have Lucy as his *fraa*.

Unfortunately, being married wasn't *gut* for his concentration. Justin had been lying under this buggy way too long, when he should have been finished by now. He slid the creeper out to work on the wheels. Maybe something that took less concentration would help his focus.

He couldn't help the curse word that slipped out of his mouth when the tool slipped from his hand and landed on his toe. He picked it up and flung it across the shop.

"*Ach*, Justin. Are you all right?" His *fraa*.

"Sorry, I didn't know you had come in."

"What's wrong?" Lucy frowned.

He jumped up and drew her into his arms. "I'm a mess, that's what's wrong."

"I don't understand."

His lips captured hers until he got his fill. "Mm...now I know why people used to take a year off after they got married. I'm useless in the shop today. You make my mind all *ferhoodled*. I lose my concentration, then I make *dumm* mistakes."

Her hand slid up his suspender and a smile formed on her lips. "It sounds like you might need a break, husband."

His heartbeat quickened when he caught desire in her eyes. "I think you're right."

He lifted his *fraa* into his arms then proceeded to the house, not caring if the neighbors were watching.

Upon entering their bedroom, his gaze caught their special bookcase headboard with their names carved into it. Lucy had loved the gift he'd commissioned Titus to make for them. She'd given him a quilt she'd made a couple of years ago for the occasion when she had no clue who she'd marry. Since they both shared a love of the color green, the quilt suited them both perfectly.

Jah, their union was truly a match made in Heaven.

SEVENTEEN

Three years later

Lucy snatched her reusable shopping bags from the pantry. "Abby, do you wanna go shopping with *Mamm*?" She eyed her daughter and husband, sitting at Abby's little table Justin had made for her. Justin looked like a giant sitting in the child-sized chair with his knees near his chest and long legs folded in two. It couldn't be comfortable, but he wore a smile nonetheless.

"Not right now, *Mamm*. *Dat* and I are having a tea party." Abby's grin stretched across her face. She always loved her daddy time, but she'd likely get less of it in a few months when her little brother or sister arrived. Their daughter looked adorable in the tiara Justin had insisted on buying for his "little princess."

Justin lifted a tiny ceramic cup between his thumb

and forefinger and took a pretend drink. Lucy laughed when she discovered his pinky finger extending up in the air. "We can finish our tea party when you get back from shopping, Abbs. I've got plenty of work in the shop to keep me busy."

Abby sighed overdramatically. "Okay."

Lucy and Justin hid their amusement. Having *kinner* was *wunderbaar* indeed. Surely, they were *gut* for the heart.

~

Perhaps it had been a bad idea bringing Abby shopping with her today. The moment Lucy spotted Trey, she cringed. She needed to get through the checkout line and out to the parking lot as soon as possible—before Trey saw them. She'd seen him in one of the aisles and tried her best to avoid him so he wouldn't notice her and Abby. Because if he did...

"Hey, Lucy! Wait up."

Oh no. Gott, *please don't let him recognize his* dochder.

She had almost made it out to her driver's van. Almost. If she could just get Abby strapped into her car seat before—

"Lucy, didn't you hear me calling you?" Trey caught up to her.

"I was in a hurry to get home." *Ach*, why wasn't her driver at the van yet? She needed to leave. Now.

He glanced into the vehicle, his eyes not leaving Abby.

"Excuse me, but we need to—"

"Is that...?" He grasped Lucy's arm and turned her to meet his eyes. "What's going on, Lucy?"

"What do you—"

He stared over her shoulder into the van. "I knew it. Something in my gut told me when I saw you at the library. I knew something was off."

Lucy frowned. "What are you talking about, Trey?"

He released her and pointed at Abby. "That little girl is mine, isn't she?"

Lucy had never been more thankful that her young *dochder* only understood *Dietsch*. "What?"

"Do *not* pretend or lie to me and tell me that is not my kid! Even with that bonnet on, I can tell. She looks exactly like me when I was her age, and I have the pictures to prove it. I don't even need a DNA test."

Lucy's mouth opened then closed.

Frustration and something else warred in Trey's eyes. "I am so angry right now." His fists clenched tight as they hung next to his thighs. "Why didn't you tell me you were carrying my baby?"

"Not now, Trey. This isn't the time or the place." She looked around, desperate for a way to escape this situation. Where was her driver?

"Yes. *Now* is the perfect time. You've kept me in the dark long enough, don't you think?" He stuffed his hands in his pockets.

"Trey, please. When I found out, I couldn't tell you. You weren't even home, you were away. You'd told me you didn't know where you were going, remember? I discovered I was in the *familye* way, and I didn't know what to do. And then my *vatter* found the test and he knew. What could I have done?"

"You could have told me at the library." His voice rose a notch.

"Why? What good would it have done? I was already engaged."

"You can get out of an engagement, you know? They're not permanent. And that's another thing." He shook his head. "I'm guessing you only married that Amish guy because you were pregnant, right?"

Ach. She shook her head. "Only at the beginning."

"So, what? Did your father *make* you marry him? Because if he did, that's considered marriage under duress. You could get it annulled, you know."

She rubbed her belly. "I don't...Trey, I'm not going to leave Justin. I love him."

126

"Get her car seat out of that van and tell your driver you're coming with me." He hitched a thumb over his shoulder.

Lucy's heart rate sped up. *Can he do that?* "No, Trey. Justin's expecting me home soon. I'm not going with you."

"Do you think I give a rip about *Justin*? We're talking about *my* baby! The one you conveniently never told me about."

"Trey, keep your voice down."

"And I couldn't care less who hears me. Lucy, what you've done is wrong." He glanced around them. "You do realize that what you've done borders on kidnapping, right?"

"What?" She could hardly breathe. Were his words true? Would they try to send her to jail? *Ach.*

"You hid my child from me for, what's it been? Three years now?" His hand raked through his hair. "Don't you think I'd would have wanted to know about my own kid? Don't you think my parents would have liked to have known they had a grandchild?"

Was this really happening? If only Justin was here with her. He'd know what to do. *Please help, Gott. Give me wisdom.* "Trey, I can't go with you right now, but maybe...maybe I can meet you sometime."

"Tomorrow. At my house. Ten thirty."

Her hands trembled as she fiddled with her collar. Was she doing the right thing, agreeing to meet with Trey?

"No, let's meet at the library instead. The last thing I need is your husband or father showing up at my house." He arched a brow. "I'm assuming you'll bring one of them along?"

She nodded.

"It's too bad you went and married that Amish guy. We could've had a good life together, Lucy." Sadness flickered in his eyes. He reached over and grazed her cheek with the back of his fingers. She pulled away. "I know I'm being a jerk, and I'm sorry. You just have to know how upset I am about this whole thing. I have a daughter." Tears misted in his eyes and Lucy's heart went out to this man she'd once thought herself in love with.

"But we talked before and you said you wouldn't become Amish, remember? I didn't have much of a choice." She glanced back toward the store to see if she could spot her *Englisch* driver. It wouldn't do for her to happen upon this situation. A married Amish bishop's *dochder* should not be engaged in an intimate conversation with an *Englisch* man.

"Tell me something. Does everyone in your Amish

community think Justin's the father of *our* baby?" Trey's frown deepened.

She nodded. "Except my *dat*. He knows the truth."

"I will never understand the ways of your people. If your father thinks it's better to sweep things under the rug, than face the truth, he's dead wrong." The steely determination in his voice made her quiver.

Her heart pounded even harder. "He was just trying to protect me and the *boppli*."

"Protect the baby from her rightful father?" His voice rose.

"No, from being gossiped about and from the ways of the world."

"So, tell me what happens in the future when I want to take *my* daughter somewhere special, like to an amusement park that's out of state? Or to the beach?"

Horror filled her heart. "You want to take her away from me? Away from the home she knows? She'd be terrified."

He grimaced. "You are not understanding me. That little girl is *my* daughter too, Lucy. I have a *right* to spend time with her and to get to know her. If we have to go to court so that I can have access to my daughter, then so be it."

This was turning into a nightmare. "Please, Trey.

She's happy now. Justin has been a *gut vatter* to her."

"She'll be happy with me too. *I* am her dad." He scowled. "And will you please stop saying *his* name? I can't even deal with this right now, I'm so angry."

"Please don't do this. I beg you." She couldn't help her tears.

"Lucy, are you all right?" Her driver, Betty, rushed toward them—finally—and threw an arm around Lucy.

Trey stepped back.

She quickly shoved her tears away. "Yeah, I'm fine." Her gaze warned Trey not to say anything.

Trey waved, acting normal. "I'll see you tomorrow, Lucy."

When he walked off, Lucy sighed.

Betty stared at her. "Is there something you want to talk about? Was that man harassing you?"

"No. I'm fine. Can we just go home, please?"

EIGHTEEN

Justin paced the living room as Lucy recounted the goings on in the store parking lot. They had put Abby down for bed early because his *fraa* had told him she had something important to discuss. Although she had tried to hide it, he'd noticed her distress the moment she returned from her shopping trip. He closed his eyes against the words he was hearing as worry seeped into his bones.

"We will take Abby to your folks tomorrow, speak with your father and ask him to pray, then go meet with Trey." It was hard to sound confident when his world around him was falling apart. He crouched in front of her and reached for her hand. He needed to be strong. "*Der Herr* will be with us."

She gasped and pointed to the window. "A car just pulled up."

Ach. Did Trey follow Lucy's driver home, so he'd

know where they lived?

"I'll go see who it is." He rushed to the door and flung it open, then sighed in relief. "It's Sammy." Just who he needed to see. *Gott's* timing was amazing.

He opened the door wide and ushered Sammy inside.

"I couldn't be this close and not stop in and say hello." Sammy's smile crinkled around his eyes. "And I brought a fresh potpie for your *fraa*."

Gott, please bless Sammy. "It's *gut* to see you. Your timing is perfect."

Sammy handed the pie to Lucy, who thanked him with a beautiful smile Justin would never tire of. *Ach*, his *fraa* was such a gift from *Der Herr*. If he ever lost her and their *dochder*, he wouldn't know what to do with himself.

Sammy must've read the angst in Justin's eyes. "Shall we go for a short walk?"

"*Jah*. That sounds *gut*." Just the older man's presence produced a calming effect for Justin. He turned to Lucy. "Do you mind?"

"*Nee*. Take as long as you need." She encouraged. She knew how much Justin admired Sammy after all the things he'd shared with her about the older man.

As soon as they were away from the house, Justin began unloading his burdens on Sammy. "To tell you the truth, I'm worried. My family is *everything* to me. I love them with all my heart. Now that Trey is back in the picture, I'm afraid I'll lose them both."

"You think your *fraa* would leave you?"

"It has been a fear of mine. I mean, she once loved him enough to create a *boppli* with him." Justin shrugged.

"But she's created a *boppli* with you too, ain't so?"

Justin couldn't hide his smile. "You can tell."

"She *chose* to marry *you*. She could have chosen him. Take heart in that fact." Sammy scratched his beard. How did he always know the right things to say? "The bonds of matrimony are strong. I don't think there's much that will take a woman away from the man she loves."

"I hope you're right."

"Don't give her a reason to leave you and she won't. I think many more marriages would stay together if men took heed to the Scriptures and loved their wives as Christ loved the church."

"I'm trying my best." But he knew he wasn't perfect.

Sammy patted Justin's hand. "*Der Herr* will work it out. You'll see. Do not fear but have faith. *And we know that all things work together for good to them that love God, to them who are the called according to His purpose.*"

"*Denki*, Sammy. I needed to hear that."

"Should we go inside and enjoy some of that potpie now?" Sammy waggled his eyebrows.

Justin chuckled. "That sounds *gut*, my friend."

He sighed in relief. Maybe Sammy was right. Maybe he just needed to place this situation in *Gott's* hands and let Him deal with it.

Because Justin had no idea how to.

NINETEEN

*J*ustin recited the verse Sammy had quoted over and over again in his mind. He'd encouraged Lucy with it too. No matter what happened during their meeting with Trey today, *Gott* was in control. He would work things out according to His will and purpose.

Justin prayed that *Gott* would give Trey patience and understanding, but most of all, he prayed that Lucy's former beau would come to know Jesus. Because really, that was Justin's main concern. If Trey knew Jesus, even if he did spend time with Abby, he could guide her down the right path.

As Trey pulled up and stepped out of his car, Justin held his breath. He brushed Lucy's forearm, attempting reassurance. "God's got this," he whispered.

Trey joined them in the small park across the street

from the library. He frowned as he neared them. "Where's my daughter?"

Oh, dear. Trey already seemed upset. Justin would need to diffuse the situation as quickly as possible. He'd do what he could to spare Lucy more angst.

"She's not here." Justin's arms crossed his chest.

"Why not?"

"It's better to discuss adult matters with just the adults." Justin insisted. "We need to figure things out between us, first."

Trey eyed Lucy. "I've already told Lucy that I want to spend time with my daughter. I'm not budging on that. I have rights. You do realize that. And make no mistake, I will keep fighting for what I know is right."

Justin rubbed his head and sighed. "We don't want to disrupt her life, to cause unnecessary stress and confusion."

"Well, maybe you should have thought about that *before* you swooped in and married my pregnant girlfriend." Trey's frowned deepened.

Ouch. He wasn't *gut* at confrontation. *Help,* Gott.

Justin frowned. "Lucy wasn't willing to marry an *Englischer*. And you weren't willing to become Amish."

"Right. But we still created a life together. And, honestly, I still love Lucy." Trey's gaze moved to

Justin's *fraa*, a sad half-smile forming on his lips.

Ach, this was not a *gut* situation. "We need to come to a solution that will work for all of us."

"My intention isn't to disrupt her life. But at the same time, I want to know my daughter." Trey stuffed his hands in his pockets like he was trying to keep it together. "I want to see her grow up."

"And how would you do that without disrupting her life?"

"I could be an *Englisch* uncle." Trey shrugged. "Unless you have a better idea."

"*Nee*, that wouldn't work." Lucy spoke up. "The community would know. And it wouldn't be truthful."

Trey snorted. "*Truthful*? Really? *Now* you're concerned about the truth. Well, then, let's just tell her I'm her real father. How's that for truth? Or is that *too much* truth for you?"

Justin stepped forward. "Maybe we didn't go about things in the perfect way, but we can't change the past."

"Right. And I'll *never* get back the first few years of my daughter's life." His lips pressed together in a flat line. "How about just a friend, then? We could meet once a week."

Justin looked at Lucy. "That sounds reasonable."

"But when she's eighteen, I want full disclosure.

She has a right to know the truth, too."

Justin grimaced. "I don't—"

Trey held up a hand. "I want my daughter to have a choice. If she decides she wants to become *Englisch*, she can. If she wants to get her high school diploma or go to college, she can. As a matter of fact, I will probably encourage her in that and put money away for it."

Lucy started to protest, but Trey stopped her.

"Those are my terms. Take them or leave them. If you choose the latter, then I will pursue custody through the courts. It's up to you to decide which you prefer."

Nee. It wouldn't do to get the law involved.

Justin squeezed his eyes closed and briefly uttered another silent prayer for wisdom. "Trey, may I ask you a question?"

He shrugged. "Yeah, sure, go for it."

"Do you know Jesus?"

"Jesus? As in Jesus Christ? We celebrate His birth at Christmas, and He died on the cross for our sins? Yeah, I know Jesus. I grew up in church."

"Do you know Him as your Saviour?"

"I accepted Jesus in my life when I was a boy. I've been baptized, even." Trey's brow lowered. "Why do you ask?"

Justin nodded. "That's *gut*."

"Listen, I know what you're thinking. I haven't done everything right. Obviously." Trey rolled his eyes. "I'm probably not the world's best example of a Christian, but I *am* a child of God. I've been saved."

Justin glanced at Lucy and raised his shoulder. "Would you mind if I spoke with Lucy in private for a minute?"

"No, go for it. I wanted to run over to the library anyhow."

They watched as Trey jogged across the street. When he'd gone inside, Justin turned to Lucy. "You're probably not going to like what I have to say, but I think we should just let Trey spend time with Abby."

Lucy's eyes flew wide. "What?"

"The *g'may* is going to eventually find out anyhow. How is Abby going to feel if she grows up thinking that we've lied to her? She's going to resent us, and then she'll rebel and go straight to the *Englisch* world. The Bible says the truth will make you free." Justin frowned. "Besides, I really feel bad for Trey. I couldn't imagine being in his shoes. I'd be angry too. I understand him needing to spend time with his daughter. She's part of him and always will be. He obviously cares for Abby. Do you think we can honestly keep her from her *dat* who wants to know her and be in her life?"

"What about my *dat*? It would ruin his reputation as a bishop."

Justin wished he could kiss away the worry that wrinkled his sweet *fraa's* forehead. "*Nee,* it won't. They might put him in the *Bann* for six weeks, but it won't be the end of the world. People realize that he isn't perfect. They'd know he was just trying to protect his *dochder,* whom he loves. And I don't plan on confessing for him. Just our part. It'll be up to your father if he wants to admit anything."

"Okay. If that's what you think is best." She reached over and squeezed his hand and her eyes held his. "I trust you."

"*Denki.*" He only prayed he was doing the right thing.

Justin's gaze flickered toward the library. "If Trey was okay with spending a day of the week with Abby, he'll be fine with every other weekend, ain't so? Especially if he can eventually tell Abby he's her father. Or maybe we should tell her first."

"*Jah,* I think *we* should be the ones to tell her. She isn't going to understand him."

"*Ach,* that's right. We're going to need to teach her English." He hadn't considered that. "We need to tell

Trey she only knows *Dietsch.*"

Lucy sucked in a breath, then released it. "*Jah*, he probably doesn't realize that."

"Can we just pray about this right now? If it's *Gott's* will, He will give us peace, right?"

She nodded and he took her hands in his. A few moments later, they lifted their heads.

Just then, Trey trotted across the street. "What did you decide?"

Justin examined his *fraa* and raised a brow.

She smiled her response.

Justin explained everything he'd just told Lucy. "What do you think?"

Trey's mouth hung open. "You're serious?"

Justin and Lucy nodded.

Tears surfaced in Trey's eyes, and he hugged both of them. "Thank you so much. You don't know what this means to me." He nodded. "And I'm going to start going to church again. I'll take Abby with me. My parents will be floored. I haven't told them yet."

"Another thing." Lucy spoke up. "She doesn't know any English yet."

"Oh." Trey rubbed his forehead. "I guess that could be a problem."

"Yes, it would. She would be frightened if we weren't there, and she didn't have a way to communicate with you. We can start teaching her and you can maybe just come to visit while she's learning. It'll give her time to get used to you and the language."

Trey nodded. "That sounds like a good plan. Ease her into the idea of me being her father."

Justin doubted Abby would truly understand at this age. He knew she'd eventually have questions. Not every little girl had both an Amish daddy and an *Englisch* daddy, after all.

After they arranged a schedule and exchanged phone numbers, Trey drove off. No doubt, he'd be on cloud nine for the rest of the week.

Justin turned to Lucy and grinned. "I think we just made his day."

She smiled. "*Jah.*"

"Let's go visit your folks and pick up Abby. We have some confessing to do."

TWENTY

*J*ustin decided he'd rather share the news with his men's group first, instead of them finding out secondhand after he and Lucy confessed before the *g'may*. Sammy had been supportive and had even encouraged him to invite Trey to their men's group. Having an *Englischer* join them would sure stir up controversy with the leaders in Detweiler's district, but it would be *gut* for Trey.

His older brothers had been surprised, but Joshua had suspected something. Justin and his younger *bruder* had always been close and not much happened with one that the other did not know. Most of the men understood Justin and Lucy's plight and didn't fault them for their deception.

Even Nathaniel Miller had been surprisingly amiable about the situation. He'd approached Justin after his confession. "Well, I've got to hand it to you, Justin. It appears you have redeemed the Beachy name."

Justin's jaw slacked. "I...what? What do you mean?"

"I'm not sure any of us would have done what you did. Stepping in to raise another man's child is a big deal. What you've done is admirable."

Justin couldn't have been more shocked. He had a hard time believing they were coming from Nathaniel's lips. "It is?"

"One hundred percent."

"Wow. *Denki* for saying that."

God's ways never ceased to amaze him. Sammy had been right. *Gott* had worked everything out, not only for Justin, Lucy, and Trey's good, but for *Der Herr's* good as well.

Perhaps He had a special plan in all this. Only time would tell what it was.

EPILOGUE

*L*ucy stared down at their brand-new *boppli*, and her heart filled with an overwhelming joy and gratitude for *Der Herr*. She couldn't help the tears trailing down her cheeks as she examined her and Justin's tiny new miracle.

"*Ach*, she's beautiful just like her *mamm*." Justin leaned on the bed and kissed Lucy's lips.

She gazed into her beloved's eyes. "I will forever be grateful to my *dat* for arranging our marriage. If he would have left it up to me, I probably would have chosen someone else."

"*Ach*! You wouldn't have chosen me?"

"*Nee*. I thought you were way out of my league. I probably would have settled for someone like Henry Stoltzfus."

"Nothing wrong with Henry."

"I know, but he isn't you. He's not a Beachy

brother." She teased.

Justin's eyebrow lifted. She loved it when he did that. "So, being a Beachy is a *gut* thing?"

"Well, I took the name as my own, didn't I?"

He leaned in for another kiss. "*Jah*, you did. And you can't give it back."

"I'll never want to."

Justin glanced up at the clock. "Trey should be bringing Abby over soon. You know she's probably dying to see her new little *schweschder*."

A knock on the door confirmed his words, and he left the room. Lucy made sure to cover herself properly.

Abby bounced into the room. "I have a sister?" She'd spoken the words in English. When they'd agreed to let Trey spend time with her, they realized she'd need to learn English quickly. She'd done a great job at picking it up, as most young *kinner* did, and was pretty fluent already.

"That's right. Would you like to come close and see her?" Lucy waved her near.

"I wanna hold her too!" Abby reached for the little one.

"I think *Dat* is going to have to help you with that." Lucy glanced up at Justin and set the *boppli* in his arms. *Ach*, he was such a *gut* father.

Justin instructed Abby to sit on the bed next to Lucy.

"But Daddy wants to hold her too. Right, Daddy?" Abby looked at Trey.

Trey glanced back and forth between Lucy and Justin. "Do you mind?"

"No, of course not." Lucy said.

Justin handed their bundle of joy over to Trey.

"I've never held one this little." Trey's eyes glassed over, and his Adam's apple bobbed. "This is a beautiful experience. Was Abby this small when she was born?"

"She was a little smaller yet," Justin said.

"Really? This one hardly weighs anything."

"About seven pounds."

Trey handed the *boppli* back to Justin. "Thank you for letting me hold her. We should probably go soon, Abby."

Justin allowed Abby to cradle her tiny sister. Lucy could hardly believe how big their little Abby looked next to their newborn.

Trey leaned against the doorframe. "I wanted to let you guys know that I met someone at church a while back. We've only been dating a few months, but I think she might be the one. How would you feel if I brought her over to meet you in a few weeks?"

Justin's gaze shot to Lucy.

"That would be wonderful." Lucy nodded.

Genuine happiness radiated from Trey's eyes.

"Abby, are you ready to go get that ice cream now?" Trey chuckled. "I had to bribe her. The baby is all she's talked about the entire day. Otherwise, she'd want to stay and hold her sister till evening."

"You're probably right." Justin smiled.

"And I'm sure Mom could use some rest, right?" Trey smiled at Lucy.

"*Jah.*" She nodded.

Abby gave both Lucy and Justin a hug and a kiss before Trey hoisted her onto his shoulders.

Lucy watched fondly as father and daughter made their way out of the bedroom. She sighed in contentment.

"Who would have thought all of this could turn out so well?" Lucy stared at her husband and *boppli* in amazement.

"*Der Herr* knew the plan all along." He planted a kiss on the little one's cheek.

"Please remind me of God's goodness next time I start doubting."

Justin lowered himself onto the bed with the *boppli* in his arms and sidled up to her. "I will, my love."

The more Lucy considered everything that had

happened, the more convinced she became that it hadn't been her father who'd arranged her and Justin's union. It had been *Der Herr* all along. He had been *The Arranger*.

THE END

Dear Reader,

I hope you enjoyed Justin and Lucy and Trey's story!

Even though what Lucy and Trey did may have been wrong...even though what Bishop Bontrager did may have been wrong...even though what Justin and Lucy did may have been wrong, God worked it all out for His glory and His good.

Aren't you so glad God can take everything we've managed to mess up in our lives and somehow make it right? What an awesome God we have!

I hope you know Him intimately. If not, you can by opening up God's Word and reading about the wonderful love He has for *you* in John 3:16 KJV. Trust Him to save you if you haven't already. You will find a peace like no other—one that can never be taken away. In Isaiah 26:3 KJV, the Bible reads, "Thou wilt keep him in perfect peace whose mind is stayed on thee, because he trusteth in thee."

One character that took me by surprise in this book was Trey. My heart went out to him. I couldn't leave him in a bad way. He needed a happily-ever-after too. One thing Trey says in this book is, "I will keep fighting for what I know is right."

I don't know about you, but I love this quote. Even when it seems like the whole world is against you, *always, always* fight for what is right. One of the best ways we can do that is on our knees in prayer. Because the root of our battles are spiritual and we need strength that can only come from God.

Thanks for reading.

To GOD be the glory!

Blessings in Christ,

Jennifer Spredemann

Heart-Touching Amish Fiction

P.S. Word of mouth is one of the best forms of advertisement and a HUGE blessing to the author. If you enjoyed this book, **please** consider leaving a review, sharing on social media, and telling your reading friends.

DISCUSSION QUESTIONS

1. If you had found yourself in Lucy's situation, what would you have done?

2. Do you think the bishop was right to seek out a husband for his daughter?

3. Poor Justin. I felt sorry for him in the beginning because he wanted so badly to clear the Beachy name—to prove to everyone that there were some Beachy brothers that stayed on the straight path and did what was right. If you were Justin, would you have sacrificed your reputation?

4. Justin is glad to have a mentor like Sammy. Sammy always seems to bring a new perspective to the table. In this instance, comparing Justin's sacrifice with Joseph, who also fathered a child that wasn't his biologically. What did you think of Sammy's illustration?

5. Do you have a mentor like Sammy in your life?

6. Do you think Lucy should have found a way to tell Trey about the baby? And if so, do you

think the two of them should have married in spite of their very different upbringings?

7. My heart also went out to Trey in this story. What were your thoughts about him?

8. The more I've thought about the characters in this story, the more I realize we can probably all relate to each one of them:

Lucy – we've all messed up and need help.

Justin – we all must make sacrifices.

Trey – we should be willing to forgive, but also stand up for what's right.

Bishop Bontrager – we all have loved ones in our lives and only want what's best for them.

Sammy – we all need a mentor and close friend to guide us in the ways of God and help us see a different perspective.

9. Did you see any other life lessons in this book?

10. Who was your favorite character in the story and why?

11. Do you know of anyone else who might benefit from you sharing this story with them?

A SPECIAL THANK YOU

I would like to express a *special* thank you to all my readers, who helped with the names in this book. Thank you to reader **Donna Montgomery Vineyard** for suggesting "Montgomery" for Trey's last name!

I'd like to take this time to thank everyone that had any involvement in this book and its production, including my Mom and Dad, who have always been supportive of my writing, my longsuffering Family—especially my handsome, encouraging Hubby, my Amish and former-Amish friends who have helped immensely in my understanding of the Amish ways, my supportive Pastor and Church family, my Proofreaders, my Editor, my Author friends, my wonderful Readers who buy, read, offer great input, and leave encouraging reviews and emails, my awesome Launch Team who, I'm confident, will 'Sprede the Word' about *The Arranger*! And last, but certainly not least, I'd like to thank my *Precious LORD and SAVIOUR JESUS CHRIST*, for without Him, none of this would have been possible!

If you haven't joined my Facebook reader group, you may do so here:
https://www.facebook.com/groups/379193966104149/

Have you read Shiloh & Mikey's book, *The Healer*?
Here's a sneak peak at book II in the **Amish Country Brides** series:

The Healer

Amish Country Brides

Jennifer Spredemann

© 2019

ONE

Shiloh Miller was sure of two things.

One, Mikey Eicher was the man she wanted to marry. Two, if her father—Silas—were to ever find out they were still courting, she'd be grounded for the rest of her life.

Which was why she now lay in her bed, as quietly as possible, waiting until she was sure and certain *Mamm* and *Dat* were fast asleep. She clicked on her flashlight and pulled out the letter she'd received from her beloved two days ago. Her eyes roamed the words for the fourth time.

> Hey, Shi.
>   I'm getting out of jail on Friday. Will you meet me at your folks' store after they turn in for the night? I'm guessing it'll be about nine or ten. I'll park my car down the road and walk to

the store and wait until you come out.
I've missed you.
Mikey

Anticipation had kept her stomach in knots all evening. If *Dat* knew she was sneaking out to meet Mikey...

~

Silas Miller couldn't shake the feeling of uneasiness. He wasn't sure what it was, but it was *something*. Like there was a storm brewing. But storm or not, if he didn't get to sleep soon, he'd be worthless in the metal shop tomorrow. And with the order he and his *bruder* Paul had to fill, they'd both need to be at the top of their game.

He listened intently to the quiet house for a moment. Nothing but the ticktock of the clock in the living room. Everyone appeared to be fast asleep. All was well in the Miller home.

Kayla slept soundly next to him. His hand ached to reach out and touch his *fraa*, but he didn't want to wake her from her slumber. She'd have a busy day too, no doubt.

He sighed, said a silent prayer, then drifted off in peaceful sleep.

~

Shiloh recalled her last conversation with *Dat* and *Mamm* about her beau. *Dat* had just come home from his men's Bible study at Mikey's *grossdawdi*, Sammy Eicher's, house. Neither *Mamm* nor *Dat* had known she'd still been dating Mikey. *Dat* hadn't been too happy that morning when he discovered that Mikey was in jail, *and* that they had been courting in secret. She knew her folks didn't approve of Mikey or his actions, but they hadn't forbidden their courtship.

Until now.

Dat wanted her to immediately put a stop to their relationship. But she couldn't break up with Mikey— she wouldn't. She loved him. And if she guessed correctly, he needed someone on his side now more than ever. How could she just abandon the love of her life when he needed her most?

She hadn't outright told *Dat* that she would *or wouldn't* break things off with Mikey. But she was positive *Dat* assumed she would obey because he'd told her to. She had never outright defied *Dat*...before tonight.

Her fingers trembled as she imagined what would happen if she and Mikey got caught. *Please don't let us get caught, Gott.*

Shiloh wasn't sure how wise it was to pray to God when she was about to go against her folks' wishes.

But she was twenty-one now. Plenty old enough to make up her own mind about who she wanted to date and marry. If only she were brave enough to utter those words to *Mamm* and *Dat*.

She shined the flashlight on her nightstand clock. *Mamm* and *Dat* had turned in an hour ago. Surely they were asleep by now. She tucked her letter under her pillow and slowly hoisted herself from the bed. Why was it that every little movement she made sounded like it was connected to a speaker, like the ones in Mikey's car?

When she reached the hallway, she stopped to listen. Sure enough, *Dat's* snore escaped through the crack under his and *Mamm's* bedroom door and echoed down the hall. If she could just tiptoe past their room, she could sneak out the front door and no one would be the wiser. Her heart pounded louder than she could think.

The moment she stepped outside, she sighed in relief. *Ach*, the fresh spring air felt so *gut*.

~

"How's the prettiest girl in the world?" Mikey drew Shiloh into his arms and claimed his first kiss of the evening.

Ach, she'd always loved his kisses. Never could

162

seem to get enough of being held in Mikey's solid arms.

Mikey's lips strayed from hers. "Mm...Shi...I wanna..."

Shiloh stepped back. "You wanna what?"

He drew her back into his arms and shook his head. "I'm not sure you want to know what I'm thinking, *schatzi*."

"I do. Tell me what's on your mind."

"I want to be with you. I want to live with you. I want to have a *boppli* with you," he murmured as his thumb caressed her cheek.

"Well, we *will* have a *boppli* eventually." She shrugged. "*Gott* willing."

"I mean *now*. Imagine if you were in the *familye* way already," he whispered close to her ear.

She was certain she must've turned watermelon pink at his bold words. She remembered her conversations with her best friend, Lucy, about how that all came about. If her *vatter* were in earshot... "*Ach*, Mikey. You shouldn't say such things. Or want that *yet*. And us not married? *Nee*."

"How do you suppose we would marry in the Amish church when it goes against my church's *Ordnung* and your *vatter* is against us?"

"I don't know." A dilemma, indeed.

"Think about it, *lieb*. It would be a *gut* thing." His

hands were warm as they gently massaged her neck. "Then your folks would insist I marry you. We'd have their blessing."

She gasped. "*Nee. Dat* would be angry."

"*Jah.* He'd get over it quick enough, though."

"I don't want to end up like Lucy."

"Lucy is happily married to Justin Beachy, Shi."

"*Jah*, she's happy *now*. But she didn't marry her *boppli's* father." She pulled back. "And you're still in *rumspringa.*"

"She would have married him if he was Amish, though. She knew she wouldn't be happy in the *Englisch* world."

"But you are? Even though you went to jail?"

"That's the thing. I didn't even *have to* go to jail. It was only because of *mei grossdawdi's* insistence. I could have gotten off with just community service had *Grossdawdi* Sammy not put his two cents in. *Dat* always listens to him."

"Don't be mad at your *grossdawdi.*"

"I'm beyond mad. I'm furious." His hands clenched at his sides

"Have you been home since you got out?"

His head shook once, and hard. "I'm not going home."

Her breath hitched. "Where will you go, then?"

"The thing is, Shi." He took her hands in his. "I want you to come with me. Please?"

"Go with you? Into the world?" Mikey was planning to leave? She pulled her hands away and tears burned her eyes. "I don't want to be *Englisch*."

"It would only be for a little while, I promise."

"What about Sierra? She'd be lost without me."

"Your *schweschder* will be fine. All your siblings will. And I know your *mamm* will understand, since she was born *Englisch*." He reached over and grasped her hand again. "And I know my *mamm* and *dat* will too. They all spent their time in the *Englisch* world, but they came back."

"*Dat* would never forgive me."

"I know Silas Miller. He's a *very* forgiving man. He might not like me right now, but he'll get over it. Everyone will."

She trembled as she considered his plan. "I'm scared, Mikey."

"You'll be with me, *schatzi*. What's there to be scared of?" He clutched her close and rubbed her back. "You know I would *never* let anything bad happen to you."

His heart beating against her ear helped to soothe her anxiety. There was something about being in Mikey's arms that lulled her senses. He always had that effect on her.

"Where would we go?" She leaned back and stared into his eyes.

"I have an idea or two about that."

"You do?" She couldn't believe they were actually having this conversation.

"When I was in jail, one of the guys told me about a place. It's a motel, but sometimes they rent rooms out."

"You...you'd want us to live together—to share a room—without being married?" She shook her head. "Mikey, I can't."

"Don't you want to be with me, *schatzi*?" He was doing it again. Those puppy dog eyes that she couldn't resist. Mikey Eicher was surely the handsomest boy she'd ever known. He was quite distracting whenever she attempted to think rationally.

"I do, but...why can't we just get baptized and join the *G'may*?"

"You know why. Detweiler's district doesn't allow courtships with Bontrager's."

"Then move here. That would solve everything, ain't not?"

"You don't understand, Shi. I can't."

"Why?"

"I've been thinking about it. I'm not ready to be Amish for *gut* yet. I have too much *Englisch* in my blood."

"But you said we'd only live away for a little while. Besides, both of your folks were born Amish. If anyone has *Englisch* in their blood, it would be me. My *mamm* was born *Englisch*."

"Which is why you're the perfect one for me, Shi." He brought her hands to his lips.

"I can't do it, Mikey. Please don't ask me to."

"But you've never even tried the *Englisch* world. How do you know you won't like it?"

"That's what I'm afraid of. What if I like it too much, Mikey? I don't want to be apart from my family and friends. Not now, and certainly not forever."

"You're not baptized yet, so it wouldn't be forever. You need to see what it's like outside of your own little world. Otherwise, you'll *always* wonder." He did have a point. "And the *Englisch* world is different than the Amish. There are no rules—no *Ordnung*—that say you have to stay *Englisch* forever. You can choose what you want."

She *had* always wondered about an *Englisch* life. And he was right. The *Englisch* had no *Ordnung* that she'd ever heard of.

"Listen, Shi. If we get married in the Amish, it will be the same way. You wouldn't be living with your family anymore and you'd mostly only see your friends at meeting. And they'll be getting married and beginning their own families too. That's just the way life goes."

"But I won't see them at all if we're *Englisch*."

"We can visit." *Ach*, why did he have to make so much sense? "And what about *rumspringa*? Even your *dat* had a *rumspringa*. I've heard plenty about the time they had in Ocean City. This would be your *rumspringa*. He won't fault you for it."

All her reasons for resisting were crumbling. "I don't know, Mikey." She nibbled on her *kapp* string.

"I'll tell you what. What if we just *try* it for a little while? If you decide you don't like it, we'll come back."

"We will?"

"But you have to give it a fair chance, okay?"

Her chin trembled. "I've never done anything like this before, Mikey. I don't want to disappoint my folks."

"Do you think they never disappointed their folks? I guarantee you they did. It's just the way of life, Shi. Our parents expect to be disappointed. They don't expect us to perfectly follow every single rule."

"I guess you're right."

"So, are you on board?"

"Only if you have a *gut* plan. I don't want to live in your car."

Mikey laughed. "*Schatzi*, I'd *never* let you live in my car."

AVAILABLE NOW in paperback and ebook at your favorite online retailer OR order direct at www.jenniferspredemann.com/shop

Thanks for reading!

Made in United States
Troutdale, OR
09/28/2024

23190389R00108